The Crisscross Crime

The black sedan veered off the main road and crashed through a chain-link fence. Stacks of cars, crushed pancake-flat, rose up on both sides of the Hardys as they followed the car.

"We're in a junkyard," Joe said.

Frank slammed on the brakes, and they skidded to a halt.

"They're bailing out!" Frank yelled as two thugs jumped from the sedan and ran. He heard a hydraulic whine outside the car. "What's that noise?"

Joe was yanking at his door handle. "I can't get my door open!" he shouted.

Frank could see that they were on some sort of cement platform. A framework of steel girders rose up on both sides of their car.

The sound outside grew louder as a dense web of cracked glass formed across the windshield. Then it exploded in on the Hardys.

"We're in an auto compactor!" Frank hollered. "If we don't get out of here, we'll be crushed flat like those junk heaps outside!"

The Hardy Boys Mystery Stories

Available from MINSTREL Books

THE HARDY BOYS®

150

THE CRISSCROSS CRIME

FRANKLIN W. DIXON

A MINSTREL® BOOK

Published by POCKET BOOKS
New York   London   Toronto   Sydney   Tokyo   Singapore

This book is a work of fiction. Names, characters, places and
incidents are products of the author's imagination or are used
fictitiously. Any resemblance to actual events or locales or
persons, living or dead, is entirely coincidental.

A MINSTREL PAPERBACK *Original*

A Minstrel Book published by
POCKET BOOKS, a division of Simon & Schuster Inc.
1230 Avenue of the Americas, New York, NY 10020

Copyright © 1998 by Simon & Schuster Inc.

Front cover illustration by John Youssi

Produced by Mega-Books, Inc.

ISBN: 0-671-00743-2

First Minstrel Books printing June 1998

10 9 8 7 6 5 4 3 2 1

THE HARDY BOYS MYSTERY STORIES is a trademark
of Simon & Schuster Inc.

THE HARDY BOYS, A MINSTREL BOOK and colophon
are registered trademarks of Simon & Schuster Inc.

Printed in the U.S.A.

Contents

1 Totaled

"Good pitching, Joe!" Frank Hardy called to his younger brother. "One more out. That's all we need."

Frank watched from his position at shortstop as Joe turned his back to the batter. He lifted his cap with one hand and wiped his blond hair out of his eyes with the other.

Frank heard their third baseman snap his gum nervously. A couple of spectators in the bleachers clapped and shouted encouragement.

"Come on, Bombers!" someone yelled.

The summer-league game had been a pitching duel from the beginning. Joe had eleven strikeouts, and the rival pitcher had been almost as good. The Bombers led 1–0 on Biff Hooper's solo home run in the fifth, but the Tigers were threatening with players on second and third with two out.

Joe carefully adjusted his cap and stepped onto the pitching rubber. The Tigers' cleanup hitter dug into the batter's box with his spikes. The barrel of his bat twitched like the tail of an angry cat.

Hiding the ball in his glove, Joe took the signals from Biff behind the plate. Frank saw Biff flash one finger toward the batter. He knew that meant an inside fastball.

Frank crouched down. Joe wound up slowly, then fired forward. Frank saw a puff of dust explode from Biff's mitt and heard the snap of the ball hitting leather. The batter stood frozen.

"Stee-rike one!" the umpire called.

"That's it, Joe. Sit him down," Frank called. "He can't even see that heat."

Biff tossed the ball back as the batter stepped out of the box and glared menacingly at Joe. He took a couple of mean cuts at the air, then stepped back in. Joe watched the runners out of the corner of his eye, keeping them close to their bases.

Frank watched as Biff flashed two fingers down—the curveball. No, Frank thought. Shake him off, Joe. Go with the heater again.

Instead Frank saw Joe nod his head slightly and adjust his grip on the ball.

Frank remained on his toes, waiting. Joe went

into his windup and released a wicked curve-ball. The ball seemed to sail right for the batter's head. Frank felt his stomach clench at the last second as the ball began its sharp arc down and in toward the plate. He expected the batter to bail out, but the guy hung in there, still as a tree.

At the last second, the batter exploded into motion, whipping the bat around. Frank saw the ball rocket toward him before he heard the crack of the bat. He dove hard to his left, extending his glove as far as he could.

Joe heard the bat slap the ball, then the gasp of the crowd. He couldn't believe it—he had just given up the game.

As he hit the ground, Frank felt the ball drive into the webbing of his glove. The power of the line drive snapped his arm back like a whip. He jumped up from the cloud of dust, holding his glove high. The ball was in the top of the webbing like a scoop of vanilla in an ice-cream cone.

The Bombers fans cheered as the Tigers' clean-up hitter threw his bat down in disgust.

The Bombers gathered around Frank, slapping him on the back.

"Great catch!" Joe said. "You really bailed me out."

"As usual," Frank teased, handing the game ball back to his brother.

After shaking hands with the sullen Tigers, Frank and Joe picked up their stuff and headed for their van. As Joe dumped the bats and gloves in the back, Biff Hooper came up, still dressed in his catcher's pads. He was sweating in the June heat.

"Hey," he said, lifting his chest protector over his massive shoulders. "How about we celebrate this victory with dinner at Mr. Pizza?"

Joe was about to second the motion when Frank cut him off. "Sorry, Buddy," Frank said. "We've got to pick up our mom's car at the repair place before it closes at six o'clock. We're late already."

"That's a drag," Biff said. He grinned. "I'll be sure to eat a couple of extra slices with double pepperoni just for you guys."

Joe's stomach growled as he watched their friend Biff and some other teammates pile into cars and take off for their favorite pizza place.

"Thanks a lot, Frank," he grumbled.

Frank tossed his cap and spikes into the back and brushed the dust off his uniform and out of his brown hair. At eighteen, he was a just a year older than Joe, but his personality sometimes made him seem much older.

"Get in," Frank said, climbing into the driver's seat. "If we hurry, we might be able to meet the guys after we get Mom's car."

"Excellent!"

The strip mall with the auto center was set back about a hundred yards from the road. As Frank wheeled the van into the parking lot, the bank and the auto center were just about to close for the day. Several restaurants were starting to attract dinner crowds, though.

"I'll get Mom's car," Frank said. He parked the van and jumped out. "Then you follow me to Mr. Pizza."

Joe nodded and slid over to the driver's seat. While he waited, he turned on the radio, running the dial through news and talk shows until he found a good rock station.

He listened to music and replayed the final out of the game in his mind. He wondered if it would help his game to videotape his pitching motion. The van was loaded with all kinds of surveillance gadgetry that the brothers used to help their father, a former New York City police officer and now well-known private detective, solve crimes. All he'd have to do, Joe figured, was set up the video camera and turn it on while he pitched. It would be great to watch himself strike some guy out with his blazing fastball.

Joe noticed a black sedan pull up in front of the First City Bank at the far end of the mall. He watched as a thickset man in black jeans and a black T-shirt stepped out of the front passenger side door and walked slowly up to the bank.

5

"Bad luck, dude," Joe said to himself. "Bank's closed."

The man pulled at the doors, then cupped his hands over his eyes and peered in through the glass. He returned quickly to the car and got in. Joe watched as the sedan slowly cruised past the van, turned, and drove out the front exit of the parking lot.

Weird, Joe thought. He turned the radio down. Looks like he doesn't want to leave.

Sure enough, a minute or two later, Joe saw the sedan again. This time it pulled off a side street and glided silently down the service drive that led to the back of the mall.

Come on, Frank, Joe thought. You may miss some excitement. He tried to see inside the auto shop, but the glare of the sunlight reflecting off the plate glass was too bright.

After putting the van in gear, he eased out of his parking space and followed the black sedan. When he got around the corner of the auto shop he stopped and jumped out next to a green Dumpster. He scooted along the brick wall, listening carefully. All he could hear was the traffic humming along the road in front of the mall.

He peeked around the corner. The black car was parked behind the bank, its engine idling. The burly guy Joe had first seen was standing on the cement steps leading up to the steel service door. He held what looked like a long tire iron in his hand.

He's breaking in! Joe realized.

After waiting four or five minutes for the mechanic to add up the bill, Frank paid it, then drove his mother's car out of the service bay. He didn't see Joe anywhere.

"Don't tell me he went to Mr. Pizza already," he muttered to himself.

He scanned the parking lot, then turned right and drove slowly toward the exit. As he passed the end of the building, he spotted their van out of the corner of his eye. Then he saw Joe, who was waving him over and motioning for him to be quiet.

Frank cut the engine and drifted up to the van. Joe ran to the open window.

"What's up?" Frank whispered.

"There are two guys breaking into the First City Bank," Joe said. "Come on."

Joe started around the back of the mall, then abruptly stopped as a piercing wail ripped through the air. At first it sounded like an air-raid siren.

"The bank alarm!" Frank shouted. "They set it off."

A split second later the black sedan roared out from behind the mall, missing Joe by inches.

"Get in!" Frank shouted to his brother. The bank robbers fishtailed out of the parking lot and shot down the main road, tires smoking.

Joe rushed to the van, grabbed his video camera, and then jumped into the car. Frank floored it.

Joe aimed the camera at the back of the getaway car, trying to get the license plate on tape. Frank wrestled with the wheel, working to keep up.

"Get closer!" Joe shouted. "I can't see anything."

Frank gritted his teeth in concentration. The black sedan wove dangerously through the traffic ahead of them.

"They're headed out of town," Frank said. "Toward the bay."

Up ahead, the sedan rocketed through a red light. The brothers watched in horror as a station wagon clipped the back of the sedan, spinning it all the way around. The driver regained control and kept going.

The station wagon lurched to a halt, steam pouring from its radiator. Frank slowed enough to make sure the driver was okay, then charged back into the chase.

Using all his driving skills, Frank crept up on the crooks' sedan. Soon he was only a couple of car lengths behind it.

The two cars next rocketed over some railroad

tracks, catching air. They hit the ground hard. Sparks shot out from under the black sedan like fireworks, and Frank had to swerve to miss the tailpipe as it flew off and bounced along the road in front of him.

Traffic thinned as they reached the town limits.

"They're slowing down," Joe said, incredulous.

Frank was right on the sedan's bumper.

Suddenly it veered off the main road and crashed through the gate of an eight-foot-high chain-link fence. Stacks of cars, crushed pancake-flat, rose up on both sides of the Hardys as they followed the black car. Stray wheels and old tires were strewn along the sides of a narrow dirt road.

"We're in a junkyard," Joe said. He worked to keep the camera focused as their car lurched and bounced over ruts and potholes. The sedan ahead was spraying them with dust and rocks.

A dim red glow appeared through the dust cloud.

"Brake lights!" Joe shouted.

Frank slammed on the brakes, locking up all four wheels. They skidded to a halt less than a foot from the back bumper of the black sedan.

"They're bailing out!" Frank yelled as the two thugs jumped from the sedan and ran. He heard a faint hydraulic whine outside the car. "What's that noise?"

Joe was yanking at his door handle. "I can't get my door open," he shouted.

As the dust cleared, Frank could see that they were on some sort of cement platform. A framework of steel girders rose up on both sides of the car.

The sound outside grew louder, moving up in pitch. A dense web of cracked glass formed across the windshield. Then it exploded in on the Hardys, showering them with thousands of round pellets of glass.

Joe held his hands up in front of his face, expecting someone to swing a bat or a club into the car. No one was out there, though.

"What's going on?" Joe shouted. He still couldn't get his door open, and now the roof was buckling. The noise grew even louder.

"We're in an auto compactor!" Frank hollered back. The doors started to press in on them. "If we don't get out of here, we'll be crushed flat like those junk heaps outside!"

2 A Scrapyard Scrape

The car shuddered as two giant steel jaws rose up on either side, completely blocking the side windows. Metal creaked and the plastic dashboard popped and crackled. Joe felt his door pushing into him as the powerful jaws squeezed shut.

Frank glanced over his shoulder. The rear window had popped out just as the windshield had. "This way, Joe!" he shouted. He leaned his seat all the way back and crawled into the back.

The rear window opening wasn't its normal rectangular shape anymore. The roof had buckled upward, turning the space into a narrow triangle. Frank scrambled out onto the trunk and reached back for Joe.

He grabbed his brother by the wrist. Joe had to

11

turn sideways to fit through the opening as the triangle grew smaller and smaller.

Without warning, Joe pulled his wrist from his brother's grasp and slid back into the car.

"Joe!" Frank shouted. "What're you doing?"

There was no answer.

Four booming explosions, one after another, rocked the car. Frank's first thought was that they were gunshots.

The car jumped, then settled back into the grip of the crushing jaws. Frank struggled to hold on. The tires had exploded, he realized with relief.

Joe's face reappeared in the opening. Then Frank saw what his brother had gone back in for—the video camera.

The space was hardly wider than an air vent. Joe reached out for help. Frank grabbed and pulled with all his strength.

Joe came free. The brothers tumbled off the trunk in a heap just as the mighty steel jaws came together, flattening their mother's car into a solid slab of metal.

Frank and Joe glanced around warily. The two crooks were nowhere in sight. All the Hardys could do was watch as the steel jaws of the car crusher disappeared into the cement platform and a huge hydraulic press came down from the framework above. The final step came when two more jaws rose up at the front and back ends of the car.

In less than three minutes, their mother's sedan had become a perfect cube of steel, not much bigger than a milk crate.

Joe filmed the whole thing with his video camera.

"That was close," he said, shutting the camera off and slinging it over his shoulder. He turned to Frank. "How're we going to tell Mom her car's now a three-thousand-pound paperweight?"

Frank shook his head in disbelief. "I say we catch those two thugs and make *them* explain."

"If we can find them," Joe said. He nodded toward the black sedan. It was parked a few yards in front of the auto compactor. "The car's there, but it looks like its occupants have vanished."

"Careful," Frank warned. "That may be what they want us to think. They might still be around here somewhere." He surveyed the junkyard. Long rows of cars stacked twenty feet high were set up in a circle around a three-bay garage. The garage was connected to a shabby structure that looked like an office. Next to the building sat a yellow crane with tanklike caterpillar tracks. A huge magnet, as big around as a pitcher's mound, dangled from the boom.

They were less than a quarter mile from the bay, and seagulls swooped and hovered over-

13

head. Except for their shrill calls everything was quiet.

"They must have taken off on foot," Joe said. He headed for the sedan. "Let's have a look at the getaway car."

As the Hardys approached the car, Joe noticed something strange. "The paint's all blistered on the hood," he said. "But the car's almost brand-new." He reached for the door handle.

The car door came open, and a terrific blast of heat and fire knocked the Hardys off their feet. Frank found himself flat on his back, watching a bright orange fireball sail up into the evening sky.

"Joe!" he called.

"I'm all right." Joe sat up a few feet away. He held his arm up to shield his eyes. Flames quickly engulfed the entire car, and the sickening odor of burning plastic and upholstery filled the air. "How'd they booby-trap the car so quickly?"

Frank stood up and brushed himself off. The flames were already starting to die down. "That was no booby trap," Frank said. "They must have set the car on fire to get rid of any evidence. But the windows were closed, so the fire only smoldered until you opened the door."

"I get it," Joe said. "Fire needs oxygen to burn. And when I let fresh air in, the whole thing went up."

"You got it," Frank replied.

The brothers walked around the car, checking

for anything the crooks might have left behind. They couldn't get too close because of the heat, but they could see enough to know there wasn't any evidence left. The thugs had even taken the license plates.

"Good thing I shot that video," Joe said. "I don't remember the plate numbers, but if we're lucky, I got the plate on tape during the chase."

"We could use a little luck," Frank said. He started toward the garage. "Maybe we can get some answers in there."

A hand-painted sign over the office door read Ron's Salvage.

Frank tried the door. It was locked. "Oh, man," he said under his breath.

"What?"

"My wallet's back in the van, along with my lock picks."

"No problem," Joe said. He jogged over to a pickup truck that had been totaled. He wrenched a two-foot-long strip of plastic from the smashed front end. Back at the office door, he slid the thin plastic between the door and the jamb and worked it up and down. The lock popped, and the door slowly creaked open.

The Hardys crept inside. Although there was still at least an hour of daylight left, all the windows of the small office were covered with brown wrapping paper, making it as dark as a cave.

"Close the door," Frank said. "I'll hit the lights." His fingers found the switch on the wall, and he turned on a single, overhead bulb.

"Cozy," Joe said sarcastically.

Frank surveyed the office. It was clean and neat, but hardly luxurious. "Yeah," he replied. "I've seen jail cells with more furniture than this."

Two large steel office desks faced the door. Each had a wooden straight-backed chair behind it. In the center of the far wall was a row of four-drawer steel filing cabinets. The cement floor was bare.

The only decorations were some old photos cut from car magazines and taped to the cinderblock walls. The tape was yellowed with age.

A huge copy machine stood against the far wall, next to the row of file cabinets.

Frank went over to the copier. "It has its own computer screen and keyboard," he noted. "Punch in a program and it practically runs itself."

"Yeah," Joe said. He lifted the document cover. "But why would a junkyard need something this fancy?"

Frank could only shrug. "Don't know," he said. "Let's scope it out." He picked up the phone on one of the desks. "But first, I'm going to call Biff and get us a ride home."

Greasy black fingerprints covered the receiver.

"Why do gas stations and repair shops always have such foul phones," Frank wondered aloud as he dialed up Mr. Pizza.

"To make you *want* to use the pay phone," Joe quipped.

Frank had Biff paged, and a few seconds later a familiar voice came on the line.

"Biff," Frank said. "We need a little help, buddy."

"What's up?"

"We're out at the junkyard on Route 6. We need a ride back into town."

"How'd you end up out there?" Biff asked.

Joe called from across the room. "Tell Biff to bring some of that pepperoni pie with him."

Frank relayed the message. "And we'll explain everything when you get here," he added.

Frank hung up and started going through the desk drawers. "Find anything yet?"

"Just some old bills and stuff," Joe said. "This place belongs to a guy named Ron Quick."

"Do you see a home address?"

"I think so." Joe found a pencil and made some notes.

Frank pushed some scraps of paper aside and pulled a large folder from the center drawer of the desk. "Hey, take a look at this," he said. "Looks like some kind of drawings or blueprints."

Joe came over as Frank undid the clasps and

17

spread the papers over the desk. "Maps," Joe said. "But of what?"

"Bayport, I think," Frank said.

Joe squinted and turned one page to see another angle. "How can you tell?"

The maps weren't like anything Joe had ever seen before. Lines of green, blue, red, brown, and yellow traced a confusing maze across the pages, intersecting, then branching off in different directions.

"It's a schematic drawing of Bayport's utilities," Frank said. "Instead of showing streets and parks, it shows all the cables, power lines, and gas lines—all that stuff."

Joe leaned over the map to get a closer look.

"See," Frank said, pointing to a jagged line close to one edge of the page. "This is the shoreline of the bay. Over here, past where the map cuts off, must be the reservoir and the dam." He put his finger on a black circle close to the center of the map. "And here's the power station."

"Got it," Joe said. "So what are maps like this doing here?"

Frank traced some lines made in orange Magic Marker. "I don't know," he replied. "But somebody's been studying them pretty carefully."

"They've even marked in some addresses and street names," Joe said. "Here's State Street, and over here is Grand Boulevard. They're both traced over in orange."

"Let's make copies," Frank said.

The paper tray of the copier was empty, so Joe focused the video camera on the maps while Frank spread each of them out on the desk.

When they were finished, Frank put the maps back into the folder and returned the folder to the drawer.

Joe motioned to the door separating the office from the garage. "I want to check in there, too," he said.

Frank nodded in agreement, but the Hardys soon discovered that the door was locked tight.

"Where's that strip of plastic I had?" Joe asked.

"I think you dropped it outside."

As Frank went to open the front door, he heard a car pull up and skid to a stop.

"Is it Biff?" Joe asked.

Frank lifted a corner of the packing paper and peered out. He looked back at Joe quickly and put a finger to his lips, signaling for his brother to stay quiet. "No," he said in a whisper. "But it's somebody almost as big."

"Is he coming in?" Joe crept over and peeked out over Frank's shoulder.

"No," Frank whispered. "He seems interested in the torched car."

19

Joe watched as a hulking figure in dark green coveralls slowly circled the wreck. The guy had long black hair pulled back into a ponytail and looked to be at least six foot three.

When the figure came around the car and faced them again, Joe backed away from the door in surprise. "Frank," he whispered. "I recognize him."

Frank raised his eyebrows.

"The dude's name is Bart Meredith," Joe continued. "Dad put him away three years ago."

"What for?"

"He took out a gas station—beat up the clerk pretty bad. I recognize him from his picture in the paper when he was arrested."

"How'd he get free so soon?" Frank asked.

"Maybe he escaped" was all Joe said.

The Hardys watched as Meredith stood nervously by his open car door.

"Looks like he's trying to decide if he should wait around or take off," Frank observed.

Joe set the camera down and reached for the door. "He's going to wish he decided to take off."

Before Frank could stop him, Joe was outside, running toward Meredith.

"Hey!" Frank called. He followed his brother out the door in time to see the big man react. All of a sudden Meredith didn't seem nervous anymore. He looked very angry and ready to fight.

Joe didn't slow down. He kept running forward as Meredith calmly reached in under the front seat of his car and came out with a heavy, four-cell flashlight. He held it up high in one hand like a torch.

Frank saw Joe lunge for Meredith. The flashlight arced down, and Frank winced at the sound—the hollow crack of metal on bone.

3 Inside Pitch

Joe was used to taking on bigger guys on the football field. As the starting halfback on offense, and middle linebacker on defense, he loved a good, solid hit. Meredith was going to go down—hard!

Then Joe saw Meredith pull out the big flashlight. Now he knew he was in trouble, but it was too late.

Joe lowered his head and lunged forward anyway. At the last second his foot hit something hard and he stumbled. Instead of nailing Meredith in the ribs, where he'd aimed, he felt his shoulder smash into the ex-con's leg.

Joe tried to keep his balance so he could drive Meredith back.

Then it was as if he'd been hit in the back with

a baseball bat. Joe crumpled to the ground, his back throbbing with pain.

Frank watched his brother fall and rushed to help. Joe's tackle had sent Meredith staggering, but the man regained his balance before Frank could get to him.

"Get away from me!" Meredith yelled. He threatened Frank with the flashlight. "Is this some kind of setup?"

"We were going to ask you the same thing," Frank growled. He was in a karate stance, ready to strike.

Joe writhed on the ground.

Meredith moved slowly toward his car. "This wasn't part of the deal, man," he said. "I don't even know who you are."

"Stick around—I'll introduce myself." Frank moved closer to cut Meredith off.

"No thanks, man!" Meredith threw the flashlight.

Frank saw the light cut through the air straight for his head. He reacted on instinct, ducking as it whirred past his ear.

It was all the time Meredith needed. He jumped into his car and floored it. The car fishtailed around and sprayed the Hardys with dirt and gravel.

The dust kept them from getting the license number.

"How're you feeling?" Frank asked.

Joe was back on his feet, scuffing his shoes around in the dirt as if searching for something.

Joe twisted a few times from side to side. "I'm okay," he said. "I would've had him, except I tripped on this stupid manhole cover." He bent down and brushed the dust off the iron disk. Lettering around the edge read Bayport Municipal Water & Sewer.

"Good thing Meredith didn't crack me in the head," Joe said. "That would've meant lights out for me."

Frank playfully smacked Joe on the back of the skull. "Sometimes I wonder if there is a light on in there."

"Bright as the sun. That's why I'm so hot-headed."

Frank laughed. "Come on. Get the camera and let's get out of here."

"What about Biff?" Joe asked.

"I'm sure he's on his way. We'll start walking and flag him down when he drives by."

The sky had turned a deep purple, and stars were starting to come out high overhead. Frank figured it had to be around nine o'clock.

The Hardys walked along the shoulder of Route 6, counting on their white baseball uniforms to tip Biff off as he passed.

No cars came down the road, though.

"How far have we walked," Joe asked after a while.

"A mile. Maybe a mile and a half," Frank guessed. "It's only two or three miles back to town."

"Biff wouldn't let us down. I wonder where he is."

Far ahead, Frank spotted what looked like the faint glow of headlights. "I'll bet that's him now."

Frank and Joe stayed clear of the road, expecting the lights to grow brighter as the car approached. The lights stayed exactly the same.

When they got closer, it seemed that one light was higher up than the other.

"Something's wrong," Frank said. "That car's not even on the road."

The Hardys broke into a jog. The second they recognized Biff's hatchback, they started running.

"Hoop!" Joe called. "Biff!"

The little car had skidded off the road and both passenger-side wheels had dropped into a ditch. The engine was still running.

Frank got there first and yanked open the driver's door. Biff was inside, slumped over the steering wheel.

Frank grabbed Biff and pulled him back in the seat. "Biff!" he yelled.

"How bad do you think it is?" Joe asked, his voice tight with tension.

"I don't see any blood."

Biff groaned and brought his hand up to his forehead. His eyes fluttered open. "Hey," he said weakly. "Hey, where's the bozo who ran me off the road?"

Frank smiled with relief. "Sounds like he's going to be okay," he said to Joe.

Biff shut off the engine, and Frank helped him out.

"Did you get a look at the car?" Joe asked.

"No," Biff said. "It was too dark. All I know is that the guy was flying—he came right at me."

"Had to be Meredith," Joe said.

Biff rubbed at a swelling knot over his left eye. "You're saying you know the clown who almost killed me?"

"He's no friend," Frank said. "We had a run-in with him back at the scrapyard." The Hardys proceeded to fill Biff in on everything that had happened to them since the game.

Biff swore to help them track down the two thugs in the black sedan. "And," he added, "when you find Meredith, I get first crack at him."

"Get in line," Joe said. He walked around to the back of Biff's car. "Frank, you steer while Biff and I push."

The three friends soon had the car back on the road, and Biff got behind the wheel.

"Watch it, Frank," he said, as his pal started to settle into the front passenger seat.

Frank glanced at the floor of the car. There, he saw a crumpled cardboard box and a circle of golden brown crust.

"Oh, don't tell me . . ." Joe moaned from the backseat.

"Yup," Biff said. "I brought you guys a hot pizza, but it looks like it took a header in the crash."

Frank gingerly lifted the pie and flipped it back into the box. The floor was covered with a wet, gooey mix of cheese and sauce.

"Sorry," Biff said.

"Don't worry," Joe said, motioning for Frank to hand him the box. "I'm not letting this thing go to waste."

Biff and Frank grimaced in disgust as Joe scooped up some loose cheese and pepperoni and glopped them on a soggy chunk of crust. He slurped in a stray strand of mozzarella.

"Mmm. Still hot," he said.

By the time Biff dropped the Hardys off at their van and they made it home, it was past ten o'clock. They found their mother, Laura Hardy, sitting on the living room couch, reading a maga- zine.

She looked up and smiled. "I'm glad to see you're home. Your game must have gone into extra innings."

Joe glanced at his older brother. He didn't want to be the one to break the news about their mother's car.

"Joe pitched a great game, Mom," Frank said, stalling for time. He clapped his brother on the sore spot on his back. "Ten strikeouts—right, Joe?"

"Eleven," Joe answered, his jaw clenched in pain.

"That's terrific, Joe." Mrs. Hardy got up and led the way to the kitchen. "Did you have dinner? Do you want a snack?"

"No, you sit down and relax," Frank said. He pulled out a chair for his mother.

Joe was already looking around in the refrigerator. He pulled out sandwich fixings with one hand and placed them on the kitchen table with the other.

Frank poured himself a glass of milk and sat down next to his mother. "Where's Aunt Gertrude?" Gertrude Hardy was their father's sister. She lived with the family, and both brothers loved her even though she tended to worry about them more than they liked.

"She's at her book club meeting," Mrs. Hardy replied. "Why?"

"Oh, no reason. Just wondering." Frank

wanted to tell his mother about her car without his aunt in the room. He could count on his mother to be calm, but Aunt Gertrude was another story.

"Your father's going to call tonight," Mrs. Hardy said. "I'm sure he'll want to hear all about the game."

"How's his case going?" Frank knew only that his father had gotten a call from the U.S. Treasury Department a couple of days ago. He'd immediately taken off for Switzerland.

"It's something about an international counterfeit ring," Mrs. Hardy said. "He's helping the Secret Service with the investigation."

"Cool," Joe said, sitting down. "Maybe he needs some help."

"You'd rather go to Switzerland than play baseball?" Mrs. Hardy asked.

"No. I want to do both. Do they have baseball in Switzerland?"

"Yeah, they play on skis," Frank joked. He watched his brother stack layers of turkey and cheese on a slice of bread.

Laura Hardy got up to get a glass of water at the sink. "So," she said. "How's my car running?"

Frank almost choked on his milk. This was the question he'd been fearing. "Well . . ." he started.

The sound of the kitchen phone ringing saved him.

Joe jumped up and grabbed the receiver. "Hardy residence."

"Joe, hi, it's Dad. How's everything?"

Joe briefly recounted the baseball victory for his father, and then went on to describe the attempted bank robbery he'd witnessed, carefully leaving out the part about the auto compactor.

He heard his mother gasp in the background. "Why didn't you say anything?" she asked Frank.

"Sounds like you've got plenty of excitement there in Bayport," Fenton Hardy said to Joe.

"Yeah," Joe replied. "Frank and I want to track down a couple of leads we've got."

"Be careful, Joe. If you find anything concrete, give Chief Collig a call, okay?"

"Will do," Joe replied. "When will you be home, Dad?"

"In a couple of days. I'm in the middle of something pretty serious. Special printing plates for fifty- and hundred-dollar bills were stolen last month on the way to the mint."

"So, why are you in Switzerland?"

"The green ink used to print American bills is made here," Mr. Hardy replied. "Two days ago a shipment was hijacked, and the Secret Service suspects a man named Larry Gainy."

"Larry Gainy? What kind of name is that for an international counterfeiter?"

Mr. Hardy chuckled. "Well, Herve DuBois is his real name, Joe. Larry Gainy is just one of his favorite aliases."

Mr. Hardy reminded Joe to be careful, then asked to speak to his wife.

While Mrs. Hardy talked, Frank and Joe went back to the living room and flopped down on the couch.

"Did you tell her?" Joe asked.

Frank rolled his eyes. "Not yet." He grabbed the remote and flipped on the TV. The evening news had just started.

"Police have not confirmed how much money was taken from the Bayport Savings Bank, but sources have informed Channel Five that the suspect got away with at least two hundred thousand dollars."

"No way!" Joe gasped, leaning forward.

As the broadcast continued, the Hardys learned the full story. The police had responded to the false alarm that Frank and Joe had witnessed earlier in the evening at First City Bank. While the police were checking that out, Bayport Savings had been hit by someone armed with a semi-automatic pistol.

"Police confirm that the robbery took place at just before six this evening," the newscaster

31

continued, "minutes before Bayport Savings was scheduled to close, and only fifteen to twenty minutes after the alarm sounded at First City. Police speculate that the thief, unable to break into First City Bank, decided on Bayport Savings as a secondary target."

Frank and Joe looked at each other. The police were wrong. The Hardys had been chasing the two First City thugs at exactly the time the Bayport robbery had gone down. There was only one explanation.

"It's got to be Meredith," Frank said, clenching his fist. "He robbed Bayport Savings, then came to the junkyard to meet up with his buddies."

Joe's eyes narrowed. "Next time we meet up with him, he won't get away so easily."

4 Caught Stealing?

Frank picked up the video camera from the coffee table and ejected the tape. "I want to see if you recorded the license number." He put the tape into the VCR and sat back down.

The tape started with the view out the windshield of their mother's car. There was a glimpse of the black sedan, then it disappeared from the frame as Frank drove the car out of the strip mall parking lot and on to the street. The picture bobbed up and down, making Joe feel almost seasick.

Their mother came into the living room and sat down just as the film showed the black sedan careening through the red light and smashing into the station wagon. The video camera had picked up the crunching sound of the impact as well.

Joe watched his mother, waiting for her reaction. But she sat quietly, her lips set in a tight line.

They could see the black sedan weaving through traffic ahead. The picture was steadier now, with only an occasional lurch or jolt.

Joe saw his mother's expression change. "That's my car you're driving, isn't it?"

Frank nodded.

"Oh, I can't believe this." Laura Hardy put her head in her hands. "And I thought you were late because the game went long."

Frank punched a button on the remote, freezing the picture. The frame stopped with the view out the windshield. The black sedan was only a few car lengths ahead. "Can you read the plate?" he asked Joe.

Joe got close to the screen. "No, it's too blurry. All we've got on these guys so far is reckless driving."

"And leaving the scene of an accident," Mrs. Hardy added. "They smashed right into that station wagon."

Frank started the film again, and the sound of screeching tires and racing engines filled the living room.

"What show is this?" a bright voice asked.

The Hardys turned to see Aunt Gertrude

34

standing in the doorway, clutching her purse in front of her. "This program looks much more exciting than my book group."

"This is just a short home movie Joe shot this afternoon," Frank said.

"Oh, my" was Aunt Gertrude's reply.

The video now showed the black sedan hitting the railroad tracks and flying two or three feet into the air. The Hardys' car followed. The picture jumped with the impact—the ceiling of the car suddenly filled the screen, then a quick flash of Joe's feet as they landed. The picture focused on the road ahead just in time to see the sedan's muffler fly past.

Aunt Gertrude sank into a wing chair, her face pale with fright. "Oh, my," she said again.

They all watched as the film showed the bank robbers turn into the junkyard in a cloud of dust. Then the picture went black.

"Is that it?" Mrs. Hardy asked.

Joe frowned. "Not quite, Mom. There's one more thing we've got to show you."

A few seconds later the picture popped on again, blurry and out of focus. Only a high-pitched whining noise could be heard.

"What's that sound?" Laura Hardy asked.

"It's called a hydraulic auto compactor," Frank said grimly.

"A what?"

Then the scene became clear. The powerful

jaws of the hydraulic press were pinching Mrs. Hardy's car flat as easily as if it were made of aluminum foil.

Mrs. Hardy held her hands to her mouth in shock. "My car," she moaned. "That's my car getting squashed flat. Were you two inside there?"

"As you can see," Joe said. "We got out just fine."

"But it was close," Frank added. "I'm really sorry, Mom. Joe and I are going to catch the guys who did this, I promise."

Aunt Gertrude stood up. "I think you should call the police right now. Show them this video."

"I have to agree," Laura Hardy said.

Joe ejected the cassette from the VCR. "But we don't have any proof, Mom. I didn't even get the license plate."

"We'll get the plate number," Frank said, looking first at Joe, then at his mother. "As soon as we get that, we'll go talk to Con Riley."

Con was the Hardys' friend inside the Bayport Police Department. Unlike Chief Collig, who was sometimes skeptical of the brothers' activities, Con respected their detective talents and would listen to their story.

It took a little while to soothe Aunt Gertrude, but soon Frank and Joe were upstairs and ready to turn in for the night.

36

"So how do you propose we get that plate number?" Joe asked.

Frank stood in the doorway of his room, toweling off his brown hair. "Computer enhancement," he said, hooking the towel over his doorknob. "We'll drop the tape off at Phil's tomorrow morning. I also want to find out what really happened at Bayport Savings Bank. One look at their surveillance video should tell us if our hunch about Bart Meredith is right."

Early the next morning the Hardys were rapping on the double wooden doors leading down to their friend Phil Cohen's cellar.

Joe was about to knock a second time when a computerized voice said, "Stand away from the door, please."

As Joe jumped back, he heard the all-too-familiar sound of hydraulic whirring. The cellar doors slowly came open, pushed up by two chrome-plated pistons.

"Radical!" Frank exclaimed.

The Hardys scrambled down the steps into Phil's basement. There, seated at his workbench, was their friend.

"How do you like my new butler?" Phil asked. He put down the soldering iron he was using and pulled off his safety goggles.

"Pretty cool," Frank said.

"If I'm in the middle of something important I don't have to get up to answer the door," Phil said.

"We've got something important," Joe said. He slapped the videotape down on the bench. If there was anyone in Bayport who could do what the Hardys were about to ask, it was Phil. He was a technical genius.

Phil picked up the tape. "You want me to analyze your pitching motion, Joe?"

Joe laughed. "I guess it's a little more serious than that. Did you happen to watch the news last night?"

Phil nodded.

"The guys who tried to rob First City Bank are on this tape," Frank said.

"Are you serious?"

"Totally. We need the plate number of the car and anything else you can get."

"Tell him about the maps," Joe said.

"Oh, right," Frank said. "At the very end of the tape, there's footage of some weird maps. We need to see those up close."

Phil nodded again. He was always ready to help the Hardys with an investigation. "Give me a few hours," he said. "I'll get you something you can use."

"We're counting on it, buddy," Joe said. "And our mother's counting on you, too."

Phil looked at Frank. "Your mom?"

"Don't ask," Frank said. "Watch the tape, you'll understand."

Their next stop was Bayport Savings. The main branch of the bank was in the middle of downtown Bayport, at the corner of a busy intersection right across from the public library, the courthouse, and the Empire Federal Bank.

No Parking signs lined the street, so Frank pulled the van into the parking lot behind the bank.

"It's showtime." Frank had figured that if they waltzed in asking questions, the bank employees would just call them a couple of kids and tell them to get lost. So the Hardys had formulated a plan.

Joe came forward from the back of the van. Although it was already burning hot out, he'd dressed like a reporter, in khaki pants, a light blue dress shirt, and brown loafers.

"Here," Frank said, holding up a navy blue tie.

Joe shook his head. "No way. I draw the line at wearing that dog collar."

Frank laughed and chucked the tie into the back. "Okay," he said. "Here's the cell phone. Make the call."

Joe flipped the phone open and punched in seven numbers. A female voice answered. "Good morning. Bayport Savings Bank."

"Good morning," Joe said. "This is Jim

39

Harper, reporter for the Bayport *Globe*. Is the manager in?"

The voice on the other end sounded wary. "No, she's not. May I take a message?"

"Is there someone else I can talk to about the robbery last night?"

"I'm sorry. The police are still investigating and they've asked us not—"

"I have information that says your security procedures were lax," Joe interrupted. He had to think of something to keep her from hanging up on him. "People could very easily have been hurt or killed," he continued. "I'd think someone there would want to answer my questions before I go to press."

There was a pause. Then, "Hold on a minute, please."

The line seemed to go dead. Joe held the phone away from his ear. "I think she cut me off," he whispered.

Then another voice came on. "Alex Stendahl speaking."

"Mr. Stendahl, hi. This is Jim—"

"Yes, I know. The voice was curt, but not angry. "You said you had some questions. Come on over and I'll be happy to talk to you."

Joe heard a click. This time the line was really dead. "I'm in," Joe said.

"Excellent," Frank told him. "Find out all you

can. If the thief fits Meredith's description, we'll know he was working a scam with those two guys we chased from First City."

Frank watched his brother jump from the van and walk briskly around to the Main Street entrance of the bank.

Around front, Joe paused to check his reflection in the smoked-glass double doors. As he adjusted his glasses, a uniformed guard stepped out and held the door open. "Coming in, sir?"

"Yes, thanks," Joe said, going in. He noticed that the guard was armed. They must be taking extra precautions since the heist, he thought to himself.

Red carpet covered the lobby floor, and the rose-colored marble of the columns matched the tellers' long counter. The first customers of the day were lining up. In the quiet, Joe could hear them gossiping about the robbery.

The opposite wall was lined with individual glass-walled offices. "Jim Harper here to see Mr. Stendahl," he said to a young woman behind a desk.

The woman spoke quietly into an intercom. Almost immediately, a tall man in a gray suit stepped out of the corner office closest to the front door. Joe noticed that he had a bandage over his right eye. "In here, Mr. Harper," the man said.

Joe stepped forward to shake hands. The man grasped his hand firmly and drew him into the office, closing the door behind them.

"Alex Stendahl, bank president," the man said. "Please, have a seat."

Joe settled into a comfortable leather office chair while Stendahl went around and sat behind his massive desk.

Joe gestured to Stendahl's bandage. "From yesterday?"

Stendahl gently touched his forehead with his fingertips. "I'm afraid so. I wish I could say I put up a good fight, but, you know . . ." His voice trailed off.

Joe smiled sympathetically. "Tell me what happened," he said.

Back in the van, Frank opened his window, reclined his seat, and kicked back. He wondered how Joe was doing inside. Getting some answers, he hoped.

His mind started to drift to baseball. The Hardys' next game was Thursday, the next day. It would be a night game, and Frank was scheduled to pitch. Frank closed his eyes. He loved pitching at night, under the lights.

Frank heard the wail of police sirens in the distance. He kept his eyes closed and concentrated on the big game.

The sirens grew louder. I wish they would shut

up, Frank thought. The sun shone warm on his face.

Then Frank sensed a shadow pass. He opened his eyes in time to see a uniformed bank guard a few steps from the van. The man had his hand poised over his gun holster.

Frank sat up.

"Freeze!" the guard shouted. "Don't even blink!"

In a blast of screaming sirens and squealing tires, two police cruisers charged into the parking lot. One skidded to a stop just inches from Frank's front bumper. The other pulled around behind.

"What's going on?" Frank asked. The flashing lights blinded him.

An amplified voice came from one of the cruisers. "You, in the van, stick your hands out the window where we can see them. You are under arrest."

5 Dog Food

Minutes earlier, inside the bank, Alex Stendahl had been giving Joe all the details of the robbery.

"The police told us all to keep quiet during the investigation," Stendahl said. "But I think it's important the public knows what's going on. They need to feel safe coming to our bank."

"Oh, I definitely agree," Joe said, taking out a pen and a small spiral notebook.

Stendahl sat forward, his elbows on his desk. "The police are almost ready to make an arrest," he announced.

Joe's jaw dropped. "That wasn't on the news last night," he almost blurted out. Then he realized a reporter wouldn't say something like that. Instead, he said calmly, "They didn't tell me anything about an arrest."

"I know," Stendahl replied. "Unfortunately it's one of our own employees. The police hope keeping things quiet will help them find her accomplice."

Joe scribbled in his notebook like a good reporter.

"Her name is Sylvia van Loveren," Stendahl continued. "She's the manager here."

"Give me all the details you remember."

"It happened at a few minutes before six," Stendahl said. "We close at six, you know."

Joe nodded.

"There were only four of us left—two tellers, Sylvia, and myself. Everyone else had gone home." Stendahl stood up and walked to the door. He gazed out at the lobby. "The guy was wearing jeans, a white T-shirt, and a black ski mask. He must've been carrying the mask in his pocket while he was outside—I don't know."

Joe kept scribbling.

"He came in through the front door, pulled a gun from the waistband of his jeans, and started shouting," Stendahl said. "I ran out of the office to try to stop him and he hit me with the barrel of the gun."

Stendahl sat back down. "I fell down. I don't remember much after that. Blood running into my eyes, more shouting. A few minutes later, he was gone."

"Is that all the description you can give me?" Joe asked. "How big was he?"

"I don't know. Pretty big, I guess."

Joe remembered that Meredith had a long ponytail. "Could you see any of his hair? Did it stick out under the mask?"

Stendahl closed his eyes for a second as if replaying the events. "No. No, I don't think I saw his hair."

"But why are the police about to arrest the manager?"

Stendahl put his hands flat on his desk. "Because this guy knew everything about our procedures. He knew there would be only four of us here. And," Stendahl said, nodding out the window at a big building down the street, "he knew Robert's Department Store had just made a big cash deposit, like they do every Monday afternoon."

"A teller could've told him those things."

"Right," Stendahl replied. "But he also knew there wouldn't be any surveillance video."

Joe stopped writing. "No video?"

Stendahl shook his head. "That's how I know it was Sylvia. She and I are the only ones who know how to operate the surveillance system. When I went to show the police the video last night, we discovered that the system had been disabled— the tape was totally blank."

"There was nothing?"

"Nothing. Well, except for the parking lot camera. She must've forgotten about that one."

Joe put the cap on his pen. "I'd like to see that video."

"I wish you could, but the police took it. There wasn't much on it—just the thief running through the parking lot with his back to the camera."

"How about a car?" Joe asked.

"No, nothing like that. The police think he got away on foot, or had a car parked a few blocks away. That's what they told me."

Joe stood up and shook hands with the bank president. "Thanks for the interview," he said. "Oh, one more question."

"Sure thing."

"Why would Miss van Loveren set up a bank robbery?"

Stendahl shrugged. "Who knows? Greed, maybe. She seems to spend a lot of money. You know, designer clothes, a sports car, things like that."

Joe whistled. "That's a lot of cake."

"Yes, it is."

They could hear sirens in the distance. Stendahl looked out over Joe's shoulder into the lobby. "Anyway," he said, going over to hold the door open. "This will be in tomorrow's paper right? Everything about Miss van Loveren and how the police are going to make an arrest?"

"Sure," Joe said. "I'll get it all in there."

Joe left the office. Through the back windows of the bank, he saw two police cars whip into the parking lot.

Customers in line craned their necks to see what was going on. "Oh, boy," a little kid said. "They found a real robber!"

"Open the door with your left hand and step out of the van!" the amplified voice boomed.

Frank did as he was told. The bank guard stepped up quickly and frisked him.

"He's clean," he said so the other officers could hear. He started to cuff Frank.

"Hold on there!" a familiar voice said. "Hold up—I know this man."

The bank guard stepped back as a Bayport officer approached. "Hey, Frank," the officer said. "You been robbing banks lately?"

Frank turned to see his friend Con Riley. "Boy, am I glad to see you. What's this all about?"

Con motioned for the other officers to relax. "There must be some mistake," he said to everyone. "Cut the lights. I'll take care of this."

At that moment Joe burst from the bank, followed closely by Alex Stendahl.

"Did you catch the thief?" Stendahl asked breathlessly. "Is that him?"

Con held up his hand. "No, Mr. Stendahl. Just a false alarm. Go on back inside, now."

Stendahl stared hard at Frank for a few seconds before reluctantly going back in. The bank guard followed him, while the remaining Bayport officers got in one of the cruisers and drove off. Con stood with the Hardys next to the open door of the van.

"Sorry about that, Frank." Con said.

Frank rubbed his wrists where the cuffs had gone on. "It's okay. But how'd I get on Bayport's Most Wanted list?"

"Your van," Con said. "We looked at the surveillance video from First City Bank last night after the false alarm. There was a van just like yours at the scene."

"Oh, man," Joe said. "So when the bank guard saw our van sitting here he figured another robbery was about to go down?"

"Exactly," Con said. "Like I said, we made a mistake. I'm sorry we gave you a scare, Frank."

Frank decided to come clean about their adventure of the night before. "You didn't make a mistake," he said. "That was our van."

Con crossed his arms in front of his chest. "Okay, fellas, out with it. I want the whole story."

Frank let Joe recount the story of the chase with the black sedan, including the miniaturization of their mother's car at Ron's Salvage.

Con looked at both Hardys angrily. "You should've called us about this last night," he said.

Joe looked at his shoes. "We wanted hard evidence first," Frank said.

"Hard evidence? This changes everything," Con said. "We thought the same guy set off the First City alarm and then robbed Bayport Savings. Now we've got two guys in a black car, an ex-con, and some junkyard owner named Ron Quick. It looks like we've either got a whole gang of criminals or just one big wild coincidence." He sucked in a deep breath, then took off his cap and scratched his head. "Are you sure it was Bart Meredith you saw at the scrap yard?"

"Positive," Joe said. "He might be this van Loveren woman's accomplice,"

"Did Stendahl tell you about her?" Con asked.

"He seems pretty sure she set things up," Joe replied.

"Well, I'm not as sure as Stendahl," Con said. "We questioned her last night but didn't get anything."

Frank saw that Con had cooled down. "We were hoping we could get a look at the Bayport Savings tape so we could see for sure if Meredith's the bank robber," he said.

"It doesn't show much," Con replied. "But I'll make you a deal. Come by the station. Bring that video of your chase and I'll see if I can get you a quick look at the surveillance tape."

"Deal," Joe said.

Con turned and strode back to his cruiser.

"Thanks for the Meredith tip," he said as he got in. "We'll check it out. And let me know if you come across anything else, okay?"

The Hardys didn't waste any time getting back into the van. "Let's get out of here before someone else decides I'd look good in a mug shot," Frank said. "Ready to get the tape from Phil? I want to see what he found before we give it to Con."

"I'm with you there," Joe said. He checked his watch. "It's only ten. Let's give Phil more time while we follow up the van Loveren lead."

Joe told his brother all the details of his interview with Alex Stendahl.

"Sounds like there's a pretty good case against this bank manager. All circumstantial, though," Frank said when Joe had finished. "It makes sense, too. A dummy like Meredith would definitely need help planning a bank job."

Joe retrieved the cell phone from the glove compartment and called information. "There's an S. van Loveren on High Street," he reported. "Take the next right."

High Street was in one of the fanciest neighborhoods in Bayport. The road curved around to a cliff high above the slate blue bay. Many of the huge houses were surrounded by stone and iron fences.

"Here it is," Joe said. "Eight-nineteen High."

Frank pulled over and they climbed out. The

51

massive redbrick house sat partly hidden behind trees and thick landscaping. Two stone lions stood guard on either side of an iron gate.

Joe buzzed the intercom and waited.

Frank pointed to a tiny camera perched up in one of the trees. "I'm getting tired of being on tape," he whispered.

The intercom crackled with static. "Who's there, please?" a female voice said.

Joe looked at his brother. "Who are we this time?"

Frank pushed the button. "This is Frank and Joe Hardy. We were at Ron's Salvage last night, and we've got some questions for Miss van Loveren."

"Miss van Loveren isn't taking any visitors."

Frank started to push the button again.

"Forget this," Joe said impatiently. He grabbed his brother by the arm. "Follow me."

Joe led Frank down the block, carefully checking for anyone who might be watching them. Even though it was now midmorning, the street seemed deserted except for a dog barking in someone's backyard.

Joe found a place where the house was completely hidden from the street. "Give me a boost," he said.

"You're kidding," Frank whispered. "We can't just climb over the fence."

"Watch me," Joe said. He leaped high and

52

grabbed the top rung of iron. With a gymnast's agility, he hoisted himself up and dropped lightly down on the other side. "Coming?" he asked, before disappearing into the foliage.

Frank sighed. Now he had to follow. As he jumped for the top, he heard the barking again and realized the dog was in the yard they were entering. He reached the top and swung over, rolling forward as he landed to cushion the fall.

Now it sounded like more than one dog—more like two, maybe three. And they were close. "Joe!" Frank hissed. "Where are you?" He heard animals running—lots of footsteps.

With a ferocious growl, a black Doberman burst through the bushes less than ten feet from Frank. In two powerful leaps it was on him, fangs bared.

6 Bad Money

Frank held his forearm out for protection. The big dog slammed into him and Frank tumbled to the ground. His one thought was to protect his neck—he knew the dog would go for his throat.

He kicked out, finding the dog's ribs. It yelped in pain, then rushed him again. Frank could smell its hot breath as it bit at him again and again.

"Off! Off!" Frank heard someone shout. "Off, Mouse! Now!"

Instantly the dog withdrew.

Frank looked up to see a young woman with shoulder-length blond hair standing a few yards away. The black Doberman now sat next to her. She held an even bigger dog at bay with a thick leash.

54

"Mouse?" Frank muttered, wiping his hands on his jeans to get rid of the dog slobber. "That's a good name for a ninety-pound dog."

"One hundred and ten pounds," the woman said. The bigger dog lunged as Frank started to get up, but the woman yanked it back sharply. "And this is Bunny."

"Figures," Frank said, checking his arms for cuts. "He looks warm and cuddly."

Bunny snarled.

"You must be Sylvia." Frank found a rip in his T-shirt, but other than that, he seemed to be okay.

The woman nodded. "And you must be somebody Hardy."

"I'm Frank." Sylvia looked to be in her early twenties. Frank guessed she'd just gotten back from a jog—she wore running shoes and a navy blue shorts and tank-top outfit. "Where's my brother?" Frank asked.

"This way." Sylvia led Frank around the hedgerow. "Are you by any chance related to Fenton Hardy?"

"He's my dad," Frank said. "How do you know him?"

"He did some work for my father last year," Sylvia said. "My father's investment company opened an office in Europe, and your father helped with background checks on all the new employees."

They stepped into the side yard. There was Joe, perched high in a tree. Another Doberman, this one light brown, sat at the base of the tree, looking up hungrily.

"Off, Lemmy!" The dog trotted over to Sylvia.

"Lemmy?"

"Short for Lemming," Sylvia said, smiling. "He's very loyal."

Frank grinned. "So loyal he'd follow you over a cliff, right?"

Joe dropped down from the tree and strode over. "What's the idea of siccing those dogs on us?" he asked angrily.

Sylvia's smile disappeared. "What's the idea of trespassing on my parents' property?"

Frank looked at his brother. "She's got you there."

Joe was still miffed. "Your parents' house? We thought this was your place."

Sylvia attached leashes to Bunny and Lemmy. "You thought I could afford a place like this?" she said, giggling. "You must've fallen on your head when you jumped the fence."

Sylvia started walking toward the house, motioning for Frank and Joe to follow. "My parents spend summers at a cabin in the mountains," she continued. "I'm house-sitting for them. In the fall I move back to my crummy apartment."

"See, Joe," Frank said. "Nothing suspicious in that."

Inside the house, Sylvia let the dogs loose and sent them scampering off.

"I overheard you guys talking about Dad," Joe said. "Just because our fathers know each other doesn't mean there's nothing crooked going on."

Sylvia froze. "Are you talking about the robbery?"

Joe nodded.

"Is your father investigating it?"

"He's in Switzerland," Frank said. "But Joe and I had some questions."

"That moron Stendahl sent you here, didn't he?" Sylvia said, leading the Hardys to a book-lined library.

"You and Stendahl don't get along?" Joe asked.

Sylvia sank into an overstuffed chair. "I'm going in this afternoon to tell him I quit."

"It's that bad?" Frank asked.

"I can't keep working for someone who thinks I'm a criminal," Sylvia said. "Besides, he treats his employees like dirt. Even though he's only president of tiny little Bayport Savings, he pretends to be some kind of jet-setter, flying overseas all the time. He leaves me to do all the work."

Frank wandered over to a shelf and looked at the books. They all seemed to be very old. "Stendahl says the bank robber had information only you could've given him."

"The police have already grilled me about

that," Sylvia said. "I didn't know anything about it."

Joe headed to an antique writing desk against the back wall. "Do you know a guy named Bart Meredith?"

"Never heard of him." Sylvia looked at Frank. "You believe me, don't you?"

Frank didn't say anything.

"I was the one who sounded the alarm. Did Stendahl tell you that?"

"No," Joe answered.

"Well, I did. Stendahl came running out of his office like a chicken with its head cut off. That's the dumbest thing to do. I stayed in mine and hit the remote alarm at my desk."

"But the guy got away," Frank said.

"Only because of that false alarm across town at First City," Sylvia replied. "If they hadn't been chasing that down they would've caught the thief red-handed."

Joe lifted up some papers on the desk. There, under the pile, was a pair of crisp new hundred-dollar bills.

"What are you doing?" Sylvia said, jumping up from the chair. "I didn't say you could dig through that stuff!"

"You always leave cash lying around?" Joe asked, holding up the two bills.

Sylvia seemed relieved. "Oh, is that what you were looking at?" She snatched the bills from

58

Joe. "Those are the newest additions to my collection."

"Collection?"

"Yeah. Here, I'll show you." Sylvia opened a file drawer in the desk and removed three or four manila folders. The Hardys watched over her shoulder as she opened the folders, revealing stacks of crisp currency.

"Wow!" Joe exclaimed. "There must be thousands of dollars in there!"

"Nope, wrong answer," Sylvia said, handing the Hardys each a fifty-dollar bill. "Care to guess again?"

Frank rubbed the bill between his fingers. "Zero," he said. His fingertips were smudged with green. "It's worthless counterfeit."

"You win!" Sylvia said, pointing at Frank.

Joe held his bill up to the light. "Where'd you get these?"

"The bank, of course," Sylvia said. "You'd be surprised how often customers come in with bad money."

"Why would someone try to pass counterfeit bills at a bank?" Frank asked. "That seems pretty stupid."

"Oh, most customers have no idea it's fake," Sylvia said. "Somebody passed it off on them and they bring it in to deposit into their accounts. They can get pretty sore when the tellers inform them they've been ripped off."

"That'd be a bummer," Joe said. "How'd you end up with it?"

Sylvia blushed. "Technically, we're supposed to send all counterfeit back to the Federal Reserve. Every now and then, though, I offer to buy the bills from the customer."

"So you *are* breaking the law," Joe said.

Sylvia cringed. "I wish you wouldn't tell anyone. If I didn't buy these, the customer would get nothing. And besides, I figure all this counterfeit is safely out of circulation here with me."

"Don't worry," Frank said. "We won't tell, will we, Joe?"

Joe dropped his bill back on the desk. "No, I guess not."

Frank picked up another hundred-dollar bill. The ink on this one didn't bleed. "How can you tell if they're no good?"

"Lot's of ways." Sylvia opened another folder. "Here's a real hundred," she said. "I keep it around for reference." She held the bill out so Frank could see it. "First of all, the green ink is a special kind that doesn't photocopy well."

"No way! You mean some people make counterfeit bills by putting money in a copy machine?"

"Sure," Sylvia said. "It's actually illegal to photocopy currency unless you enlarge it at least one hundred and fifty percent."

"Wild," Frank said. "What else?"

Joe tried to act as if he wasn't interested, but found himself creeping closer to watch. "They make that ink in Switzerland," he said, remembering his phone conversation with his father.

"That's right!" Sylvia said. "I'm impressed."

"I know a few things," Joe said.

"How about this?" Sylvia asked. She tilted the bill in the light. The number "100" in the lower right-hand corner shifted from green to black.

"Cool," Frank said. "It's like a hologram."

Sylvia then opened the center drawer of the desk and found a magnifying glass. She handed it, along with the bill, to Frank. "Look at Ben Franklin's collar," she instructed.

Frank held the glass close. "Joe, you've got to see this. There are tiny words written on old Ben's collar. It says, 'United States of America.'"

"It takes amazing engraving to make words that small," Sylvia said. "Here." She took the bill back and held it up to the light. "Here's the last thing."

Frank looked at the spot where Sylvia's thumb was pointing, an inch or so to the right of the portrait. There, imbedded in the paper of the bill, was a yellow ribbon only about a sixteenth of an inch wide. On it, tiny letters spelled out "USA 100," followed by a little American flag.

"That ribbon is on twenties and fifties, too,"

61

Sylvia said. "It's called micro-coding, and it's woven right into the paper." She turned to Joe. "You know where the paper comes from, smart guy?"

Joe shook his head.

"Canada. In fact, the government stores the micro-coded paper right here in Bayport before they ship it out to the mints. Pretty neat, huh?"

Joe dismissed Sylvia with a wave of his hand. "Yeah, totally neat," he said sarcastically. "Thanks for the lesson, but now it's time for lunch." He started for the door.

Frank apologized for Joe's rudeness. "We'll let you know when we learn something new," he said, following his brother out.

Joe was already sitting in the driver's seat when Frank got to the van. "You think she's telling the truth, don't you, Frank?" he asked.

Frank handed Joe the keys. "Why would she trip the alarm if she was involved in the robbery? It's not logical."

"It is if she knew the cops would be delayed because of the false alarm at First City," Joe countered.

Frank didn't have an answer to that.

"We should keep an eye on her," Joe said. "Meanwhile, let's grab a sandwich and then get over to Phil's."

After a quick lunch at home, the Hardys

62

jumped back into the van. As they backed out of the driveway, Joe noticed a white pickup truck parked against the curb a block away. What neither Hardy noticed, when Joe put the van in drive and took off down the street, was the pickup truck that pulled away from the curb and followed them.

7 Vanishing Act

Ten minutes later Joe pulled the van up in front of Phil's house. A couple of times along the way he'd seen a pickup truck a few cars behind them. Now he checked the side mirrors. He didn't see the truck anymore.

"What's up?" Frank asked as he got out of the van.

Joe glanced up and down the street. "Nothing," he said. He joined his brother on the sidewalk. "I thought somebody might be following us. Just getting paranoid, I guess."

Down in the basement, the Hardys found Phil sitting in front of an oversize computer monitor. "Guys, check out the shots I got."

Frank and Joe gathered around the monitor. "What is all this stuff?" Joe asked. He marveled at the jumble of electronics and the tangle of wires.

"This," Phil answered, pointing to a machine that looked like a double-size VCR, "is a digital effects recorder. I can freeze one frame at a time on your video with this."

"We already tried that with our VCR," Joe said. "The picture was too blurry."

"Right," Phil answered. "This machine digitizes the image."

"Digitizes it?" Joe asked.

"Yeah," Frank said. "It means it stores the picture as numbers."

"Like one of those kids' coloring books that says, 'Everywhere you see the number one, color in blue; where you see number two, put in green . . .' like that?" Joe asked.

"Exactly," Phil said. "Then I transfer the digitized image to a compact disk and ask the computer to fill in the right numbers where some are missing. So everywhere the computer sees numbers that correspond to blue, it adds a little more blue until I tell it to stop, and so on."

"Got it," Joe said. "Turn on the show."

Phil punched in some numbers on a keyboard, telling the CD-ROM to search for a certain image on the disk. The machine buzzed for a second, then a picture popped up on the computer screen.

At first, the picture was no better than it had

been on the Hardys' VCR. Gradually, though, the image became clearer as the computer added more detail.

"Nice!" Joe exclaimed. The picture showed the black sedan charging down the street twenty or thirty yards ahead of the Hardys in their mother's car. But now the license plate was clearly visible.

Phil printed the image.

"Did you find any frames with good pictures of the guys in the car?" Joe asked.

"Nope," Phil replied. "We never see anything more than the backs of their heads." Phil handed Frank the printed page. He picked up another stack of papers. "I already printed the pictures of those maps you guys filmed."

Frank spread the papers out on Phil's workbench. With the pages in the right order, an almost complete map of Bayport was made. "What do you make of it?" he asked Phil.

Phil rubbed his chin thoughtfully. "The red lines are definitely the electrical and phone lines—"

"And these green lines that come from the power plant west of town," Frank added, "must be the gas lines."

Phil nodded. "Where are the waterworks?"

"Here." Joe placed a finger on some black circles close to the bay. "This is the sewage treatment plant."

"So the blue lines are fresh water going out, and the brown lines are sewage going back to be treated."

"And the yellow?" Joe asked. "Somebody was pretty interested in them." There weren't as many yellow lines as those of the other colors, but whoever had been studying the maps at Ron's Salvage had traced over a lot of them with an orange highlighter to make them stand out clearly.

The three stared at the map, concentrating.

They all jumped when the sound of Phil's new doorbell broke the silence. "Stand away from the doors, please," the voice commanded loudly.

Phil glanced at the Hardys, then up at the double cellar doors. "Who's there?" he called.

A crack of sunlight shot in as someone tried to pull the doors up and open.

"I said, who's there?" Phil shouted.

The doors slammed shut.

"Open them," Frank whispered. He and Joe quietly padded to positions next to the steps so they could see out when the doors were opened. When Frank signaled, Phil pushed a button.

The doors slowly pushed open.

No one was there—just a wide square of cloudless blue sky.

Frank pointed up.

Joe nodded, his jaw set. They'd have to go up. He started up the stairs slowly.

After three or four steps, his head was high enough for him to see out into Phil's backyard. It was empty.

He took a few more cautious steps up. "Must've been some neighborhood kid goofing on us," he said.

Joe took another step, and it was as if a thick rope had been noosed around his neck. He brought his hands up—he couldn't breathe! He tried to say Frank's name, but nothing came out.

He saw the sky, the blue darkening at the edges. Then he felt himself being lifted, then dropped, on the soft grass of Phil's lawn.

From down in the basement, Frank had seen a dark figure rise up from behind one of the open doors. A thick arm had snaked around Joe's neck, and then Joe had disappeared from view.

Frank rushed up the steps. "Meredith!" he said. "Let him go!"

The big ex-con had Joe down on the lawn, holding one arm pinned behind his back.

Frank had revenge in his eyes as he started for Meredith.

"I'll break it," Meredith shouted. He pushed up on Joe's arm and Joe groaned. "Come any closer, and I'll do it!"

Frank stayed back. "What do you want, Meredith?"

"I had a visit from the cops this morning," the

big man said. "Seems *somebody* accused me of robbing Bayport Savings."

Joe spit out some grass. "You're going back to jail, Meredith."

Meredith pulled on the arm some more.

"I did my time," the ex-con said. "I got a real job now, and I'm not gonna let two punks like you mess it up."

"If you don't let my brother go, assault will be added to the robbery charges," Frank said.

Meredith's face twisted in anger. "I'm telling you I'm clean," he shouted. "This is a warning—get off my case!" He glanced around. "Are those sirens? Who called the cops?"

"I did," Phil said as he came up from the basement.

Meredith jumped up, releasing Joe. He bolted for the street.

In a flash Frank was after him. With his sprinter's speed, Frank caught up to Meredith quickly. He was about to make a diving tackle, when Meredith vanished from view.

What? was all Frank had time to think before he went flying head over heels. He almost did a full flip in midair before landing flat on his back.

It was all the ex-con needed. He leaped into the white pickup and floored it, sending up a purple cloud of burned rubber.

Frank jumped up and ran to the curb, but all he could do was watch as the truck disappeared around the corner. Frank's temples pounded with rage as he realized what had just happened. Meredith had suddenly dropped to the ground as they ran, causing Frank to trip over the man. "I can't believe I fell for such an amateur trick," he muttered to himself.

Joe and Phil jogged up to him then.

"He got away," Frank told them. "But the truck he was driving said Ron's Salvage Yard on the side."

"He also left this behind," Joe said. He held out a wallet. "Take a look inside."

Frank took the wallet and opened it. He pulled out six crisp, new one-hundred-dollar bills.

"Hold them up to the sun," Phil said.

Frank fanned the bills out like playing cards and held them up. "So much for his story about being innocent," he said. Not one of the bills had the yellow, micro-coded strip. They were all fake.

Frank pocketed the wallet before the police arrived a few seconds later. He, Joe, and Phil took turns explaining what had happened.

"You okay?" one of the officers asked Joe.

Joe lifted his arm, stretching his shoulder. "I'm fine," he said. "But Meredith's not going to be when I catch up to him."

"Listen," the officer said, pointing his pen at Joe. "You leave him to us, understand?"

Joe didn't say anything.

A call came over the officer's walkie-talkie. After a short exchange, he nodded and put it back on his belt. "Con Riley wants to see you two at the station," he said. "You can either ride with me or follow in your van."

Joe figured they must be in trouble for something, though he couldn't figure what. "We'll follow," he said glumly.

At the station, an office led the Hardys into an empty interrogation room. "Officer Riley will be in to see you in a few minutes," he said, shutting the door as he left.

The Hardys sat at a steel table. "So what was Meredith doing with counterfeit hundreds?" Joe asked in a low voice.

"I don't know," Frank whispered.

"I'll bet he got them from Sylvia. They're exactly like the bills she had, and that would make them accomplices, just like I said."

Frank was about to take the wallet out and look at the cash when Con Riley came in, pushing a cart with a TV and VCR. He also had two cans of soda, which he handed to the Hardys.

"Here," he said. "Have a drink."

"Thanks," Frank and Joe said in unison.

Con sat down across from the Hardys. "Bring that tape with you?" he asked.

"Even better," Joe said, pulling a folded paper from his jeans pocket. "This picture shows the plate number perfectly."

71

Con took the photo. "Great. I'll look it up on the computer." He took a videotape and put it in the player. "Now here's my part of the deal."

"The surveillance tape from the bank?" Joe asked.

"Yup. Here's the shot of the parking lot."

Con and the Hardys watched the grainy black-and-white film. White numbers in the lower right hand corner counted off the seconds as the camera slowly panned back and forth across the lot.

"It's quick," Con said. "Watch closely. There!" He pointed to the screen.

Frank and Joe watched a man enter the picture from the bottom of the frame, his back to the camera. A few seconds later the camera panned away.

"That's all you got?" Joe asked.

"Keep watching," Con said. "You'd expect to see him again when the camera turns back, but . . ."

They watched in silence as the camera panned back across the parking lot. The man was gone.

"It's like he went up in thin air," Con said. "One second he's walking along, three seconds later he's nowhere to be found." He shrugged. "That's it." He stopped the tape and started to get up.

"Nuts!" Joe said. "You can't tell from that if it's Bart Meredith or someone else."

Con settled back in his chair.

"I heard you had another run-in with him. I told you we'd take care of talking to him."

"He found us," Frank said. "He had a charming way of trying to convince us that he's innocent."

"He is innocent," Con said.

Joe pounded his fists on the table and stood up. "Are you kidding me?"

Con shook his head. "He's got an alibi. He was at work, waxing the floors of the courthouse, when the robbery happened."

"He works in the courthouse?" Joe asked in disbelief.

"He's a janitor for the company that cleans all the city buildings," Con said. "They say he's a great employee."

"What about the fact that I saw him driving a truck from Ron's Salvage?" Frank asked. "The two guys who tried to rob First City have something to do with that junkyard. When we followed them they led us into that auto compactor on purpose, and Meredith is *definitely* connected to them. We just don't know how."

Con's expression changed. "He was driving Ron Quick's truck, you said? A white pickup?"

Frank nodded.

Con looked worried. "Ron Quick's wife called a little while ago. She said her husband's been missing for two days."

8 Biff Calls the Plays

Frank's eyebrows shot up. "Two days? She didn't call until now?"

"She said he sometimes works so hard that he sleeps on a cot at the scrapyard," Con said. "When he didn't call, she went over there. She says there's a new lock on the gate. She couldn't get in."

"He's either working with Meredith or in big trouble," Joe said.

Con got up. "We'll find out soon," he said. "We sent a cruiser over to see what's going on." He left to go punch the plate number into the computer.

Another officer came in while the Hardys waited. She plopped a stack of books, each as thick as a dictionary, down on the table. "Con

74

says you got a look at one of the guys who tried to break into First City," she said to Joe. "Flip through these mug books. See what you can see."

Joe's shoulders sagged. "Sure," he said. When the officer left, he shoved half the books over to Frank. "Look for a dude with a buzz cut," he said, remembering the man he'd seen get out of the black sedan and peek into the First City bank window. "Dark hair, square chin, thick neck, like a wrestler."

For the next fifteen minutes, the Hardys flipped through pages and pages of mug shots. Every minute or so, Frank would turn his book toward Joe and ask, "Is this the guy?"

Joe would shake his head. "No, look for bigger eyes," he'd instruct. Or, "Watch for a nose that looks like it's been busted a couple of times."

Finally Con came back in, holding a computer printout. "Any luck?" he asked.

"No," Joe said, closing a book. "Plenty of ugly mugs in here, though. What'd you get?"

"Got a hit on that plate," Con said. "The car's registered to Speedy Rent-a-Car. I called and they said they rented that car yesterday morning to a guy named . . ." Con glanced at the printout. "A guy named Earl Galatin."

"Cool," Joe said. "You get an address?"

Con smiled apologetically. "We're already checking it out," he said. "Chief Collig says,

75

'Thanks for the information, but stay clear of the investigation from now on.'"

"Figures," Joe said. He pushed his chair back from the table. "Let's get out of here, Frank. Chief Collig wants us to go home and bake cookies or something."

The door to the interrogation room opened and the officer stuck her head back in. "No news, Con," she said. "Unit fifteen just got back from Ron's Salvage. They didn't find anything—no evidence of foul play."

Con nodded. "Thanks."

"Wait," Frank said. He'd suddenly remembered what Sylvia van Loveren had said about people photocopying currency. "Did they say anything about the copy machine in the office?"

The officer got a funny look on her face. "Yeah, they did. Mrs. Quick said her husband was having money troubles, but almost the only thing in his office was a brand-new copy machine that must've cost like around fifty grand. How'd you know?"

Frank shrugged. He didn't want to say too much until he had things figured out. "We saw it yesterday. Seemed a little strange to us, too."

The officer left and Joe started to get up to go. As Frank stood, he flipped through one more page of the mug book.

"Hold on," he said, pushing the book over to Joe. "How about him?"

Joe leaned forward, studying the photo. "That's him," he said. "That's the guy I saw."

Con looked at the photograph in silence.

"Who is he?" Frank asked.

Con let out a deep breath. "You might be right about Bart Meredith after all," he said. "That's Eddie Racine. He was Meredith's cellmate in prison. Got out a few weeks ago."

The Hardys looked at each other. "I knew it," Joe said. "No way Meredith had an alibi for the robbery."

Frank pointed a finger at Joe. "So, Eddie Racine was in the car, and Meredith robbed Bayport Savings . . . but who was the driver of the black car? It must be this Earl Galatin guy, right?"

"Don't forget Sylvia van Loveren," Joe said. "It had to be her giving them inside information." He looked up at Con. "I'd say we're about to close another case."

Frank wasn't so sure. He had six fake bills in his pocket from Meredith, and there was the copy machine. Why would bank robbers be involved in counterfeiting?

Con suddenly turned back toward the door. Frank and Joe heard the same thing he did—lots of commotion outside.

An officer burst into the room. "Con!" he shouted. "Come on! The alarm's going off at Empire Federal!"

Con sprinted out. "Which branch?" he called.

The Hardys heard the other officer's answer. "Out on Ridge Road." Then the voices were lost under the clamor of slamming car doors and gunning engines.

No discussion was needed. "I'll drive," Frank said as the brothers rushed to the van to join in the chase.

Frank bounced the van over the curb and into the street in hot pursuit of three or four police cruisers.

"They're taking Smith Street north," Joe said. "That must be the quickest way to Ridge."

Passenger cars up ahead pulled over to let the police cruisers fly past. The Hardys followed before the opening in traffic closed.

"I could use blocking like this in football games," Joe joked.

"You'd get a lot more yards if you didn't trip over your own shoelaces," Frank teased. He cut the wheel hard to the left, keeping a safe distance as the screaming cruisers up ahead pitched single file onto Ridge and roared up the street.

Frank's tone got serious. "Answer the phone," he said.

"What?"

"The phone, it's ringing."

"Oops, didn't hear it." Joe flipped open the cell phone. "Yes?" he said loudly, his finger in his free ear to block out the sirens.

"Joe, it's Biff. You got to get over here, man."

"We're kind of in the middle of something," Joe shouted.

Biff's voice sounded urgent. "I'm downtown," he said. "At the sub shop. There's a freaky-looking guy across the street, and I'm positive he's casing out Empire Federal."

"Are you sure?"

"Joe, I'm not imagining things. You've got to get over here. I called the cops, but they blew me off."

"Hang tight," Joe said, flipping the phone closed.

"Turn around," he said to Frank.

"What're you talking about? We're almost there."

"I think the police are headed to the wrong branch of Empire Federal," Joe said. "Biff spotted somebody casing the downtown branch."

Frank had to make a decision. If they quit following the police now, they would miss out on what was happening at the Ridge Street branch. "Biff says he saw something suspicious? That's all we're going on?"

Joe nodded.

Frank clenched his jaw and hit the brakes. As the van skidded to a stop, he wrenched the wheel around and gunned the engine. Seconds later they were headed back in the direction they had come from—toward downtown Bayport.

"I hope Biff's right," Frank said.

Downtown, everything seemed strangely quiet compared to the wailing of the police sirens. Frank pulled the van to the curb about half a block from the sub shop.

The Hardys got out, acting casual, then walked over to meet Biff. Without being too obvious, they glanced over at the stately, four-story stone building that housed the downtown branch of Empire Federal Bank. Few other people were out on the sidewalks in the midafternoon heat, and the Hardys didn't see anyone outside the bank.

They found Biff sitting at a window booth in the sub shop. From there he had a clear view of the front entrance to the bank.

"Okay," Frank said, settling into the booth. "What's up?"

Biff leaned forward, his huge shoulders hunched up by his ears. "He was over there, I swear."

Joe threw up his hands. "You mean he's gone now?"

Biff looked embarrassed. "He was really creepy looking, Joe. He had thick red hair, you know. It was, like, all over the place. And he had sunglasses and a mustache."

"What's so creepy about that?"

"It all looked fake, like the hair was a wig. The mustache didn't look right either."

"Hey," Joe said, under his breath. "That must be him."

Frank and Biff followed Joe's gaze out the window. They watched as a redheaded man dressed in a cheap-looking business suit stepped out of an alley between a jewelry store and the bank.

"That's him!" Biff confirmed.

The man stopped outside the bank doors. He glanced around before quickly disappearing inside.

Joe jumped up. "Yeah, he looks like he's about to make a mighty big withdrawal."

"Be cool," Frank warned as he and Biff followed Joe out. "We don't want to make a mistake and bust some guy for just looking funny."

"Don't worry," Joe said. "If looking funny were a crime, you'd get a life sentence."

Biff chuckled out loud.

The three friends crossed the street quickly, then slowed as they carefully approached the bank. With the afternoon glare, they couldn't see anything through the smoked-glass windows. The street was nearly deserted.

"Here's what we do," Frank whispered. "I'll walk in like a regular customer. If there's nothing wrong, I'll act like I forgot something and walk right back out. If I don't come out in ten seconds, you know something's up. Call the police."

Joe and Biff nodded.

Frank set his facial expression on neutral, just a normal guy running a bank errand. Then he walked through the first set of double doors.

Pausing in the space between the two sets of doors, he felt a cool breeze from the bank's air-conditioning. Trying to see through the second set of doors, he thought he could make out the shapes of people moving around inside. Things looked normal enough.

He pushed through the second set of doors and into the bank. The sight inside sent a chill down his spine.

Five or six bank customers lay on the floor, their hands clasped behind their heads.

Two tellers rushed around behind the counter, dumping trays of cash into a cloth satchel. One of them sobbed quietly as she worked.

The redheaded man stood in the center of the room, a gun raised over his head.

He spotted Frank instantly. "Get down!" he shouted. He took a step toward Frank and brandished the gun in his direction. "Get on the floor—now!"

9 Hit Batsman

Outside, Biff and Joe waited. The seconds ticked past.

"Something's wrong," Joe said. "We've got to get in there."

Biff put his hand on Joe's shoulder. "Frank said to call the cops and wait."

"No," Joe said. "That could take too long. Frank might be in trouble." He took off, leaving Biff with a bewildered expression on his face.

Joe sprinted across the street to the van. He yanked the sliding door open and pulled out two baseball bats.

A woman coming out of an ice-cream store stopped and stared at him.

"Call the police!" Joe called to her as he ran

back across the street. "Empire Federal's being robbed."

The woman dropped her yogurt to the sidewalk and dashed back inside the ice-cream store.

Joe tossed a bat to Biff. "I'll go around to the side," he said. "Give me ten seconds, then go in the front, fast."

Joe ran to the side entrance, counting to himself. He barely had time to catch his breath before he reached ten. Lowering his shoulder, he slammed into the door, hitting it so hard that it swung back into the wall. The glass shattered, showering the floor with tiny glass pellets.

Inside, Frank had done as he was told and was lying on the floor, his fingers locked behind his head.

He felt the redheaded man looming over him, making sure he was complying. When Frank saw the man's shoes start to move the other way, he peeked up, hoping to memorize something about the robber that would help in capturing him later.

The man spun around suddenly. "Keep that head down!" he yelled. Then he spoke to everyone in the bank. "You all stay nice and quiet," he said. "This will all be over in a few minutes."

At that moment Frank heard a terrific crash. He looked up to see Joe stagger in, covered with round pellets of glass.

84

Startled, the crook held the gun out in two hands, pointed right at Joe. Then Frank saw him turn to the front door. There was Biff!

Biff held the bat ready to swing and took a step toward the robber.

"Biff! He's got a gun!" Frank shouted.

Biff froze.

Frank heard the gun go off. An awful orange flash lit up the bank.

The bullet ripped through the barrel of Biff's bat, exploding it into a confetti of wood chips. For a split second, Biff stood holding just the handle of the bat, then he dove for cover behind a desk.

Joe saw his chance. He blitzed the thug, swinging his bat at the guy's wrists. He hit the gun, and it went skittering across the tile floor.

The redheaded man started to go for the gun, but Frank was already up, blocking his path to the weapon.

"Come and get it," Frank said, beckoning the man with a wave of his hand.

After a second's hesitation the crook turned and fled through the rear emergency exit. The Hardys pursued him into the parking lot.

Running at full speed, Joe swung the bat, hitting the man on the side of his leg. The crook tripped and tumbled forward.

Joe went in to finish him off, but the thug was up in a flash, ready to fight.

Frank circled to the man's right, while Joe took a step to his left.

"You'd better give it up," Joe warned, holding the bat out menacingly. "I don't want to have to hurt you."

The thug grinned. He reached into the lining of his suit coat and withdrew a steel crowbar. "Now it's your turn to bring it on," he said.

Unfazed, Joe took a swing. The man held out the crowbar. There was a loud *thock!* as wood and steel collided. Joe's hands rung with pain.

Frank took a chance. While the man's back was turned, he stepped in, planning to bring the guy down with a side kick to the back of his knee.

The thug was too quick.

As Frank's leg shot out, the man spun and nailed him right in the shin with the crowbar.

Frank yowled and crumpled to the ground.

The thug turned and ran toward the alley. Joe rushed to his brother's side.

"I'm okay," Frank said through gritted teeth. "Go after him, Joe!"

Joe sprinted to the mouth of the alley. It was completely empty. He ran to where it opened up on State Street, across from the sub shop. He looked right and left. No sign of the redheaded man.

A white-haired woman stood waiting at the bus stop a few yards away.

"Did you see a guy running out here a few seconds ago?" Joe asked.

The woman looked at Joe, then at his baseball bat. "No," she said. Then she began scolding Joe. "You shouldn't be playing baseball back in that parking lot," she said. "There are parks for that kind of thing, you know."

Joe sighed. "I know," he said. "Thanks."

He headed back through the alley. Stopping in the middle, he looked up. No fire escapes, no way to climb up to the roof, he thought. The guy had just vanished, inside an alley.

He tapped the barrel of the bat along the pavement as he headed back to Frank. He noticed that the sound had changed pitch. Looking down, he saw that he'd struck a manhole cover a lot like the one he'd tripped over in the junkyard. Well, he thought, at least I didn't take a tumble over this one. Then he had an idea. Reaching down, he tried to get his fingers under the rim of the lid to lift it up.

"No way," he muttered, almost tearing off his fingernails. "This thing must weigh close to two hundred pounds. No way to get it up without some kind of help."

Back in the parking lot, he found Biff helping Frank up.

"How's the leg?"

Frank pulled up the leg of his jeans, revealing

87

an egg-size welt. He tested the leg, walking slowly in circles. "I'll live."

"Where'd the guy go?" Biff asked.

Joe rested his bat on his shoulder. "No idea. Went into the alley and then"—Joe snapped his fingers—"vanished. He didn't look nearly big enough to be Meredith, though."

Frank stamped his pants leg back into place. "This time it must've been Racine or Galatin wearing a wig, like Biff figured." He walked gingerly to the bank door. "I want to get back inside the bank and ask some questions," he said.

The Hardys and Biff found most of the customers gathered in a clump next to the teller line. They were hugging one another and talking loudly about the adventure they'd just shared.

The crook's gun still lay in the middle of the floor, and Frank asked Biff to make sure no one touched it.

Behind the counter, the bank manager and several other employees tried to comfort the teller who'd been crying before.

Frank and Joe asked a few questions, but the customers had either been too scared to take a close look at the robber or were now too upset to talk about it.

Joe was about to go over to talk to the employees when a deep voice called his name from across the lobby.

"Joe Hardy! What are you doing here!"

It was Chief Collig, leading a troop of five or six officers. While one officer swooped down on the gun, Collig came straight up to Frank and Joe. "I've had enough of your interference in this investigation," he said, poking an index finger into Joe's chest. He turned to Frank next. "You're supposed to be the older, more responsible one. What were you thinking coming in here like cowboys? You could've gotten hurt. These innocent people could've been killed!"

The bank manager strode around from behind the counter. "Please!" she said. "I have something to say."

Collig stared at her, his face red with anger.

"Thanks to these young men, we're all safe," the manager said firmly. "The thief didn't even get any money. What I'd like to know is why it took you so long to get here after I pushed the alarm."

Joe didn't think Chief Collig's face could get any redder, but it did. "Humph" was all Collig said before turning abruptly to give orders to his officers. When he finally had himself composed, he apologized to the manager—but not before he told the Hardys and Biff to get out of his sight.

Joe was happy to follow the chief's orders.

"I've got to get home," Biff said.

Frank and Joe said goodbye to their friend,

then walked over to find Con Riley using the manager's key ring to get into a back storage room.

"False alarm out on Ridge?" Frank asked.

"That's right," Con said in a whisper. "A little bit different from yesterday, though." He tried another key. "The manager out there said that two men walked into the bank wearing black ski masks. One watched the customers while the other went into the manager's office and demanded that he push the alarm button."

"No way!" Joe said.

"Yup. The guys were cool as cucumbers, the manager said. They stood around for two or three minutes—just long enough for us to get close— then took off."

Con finally found the right key and got the room open. Frank and Joe followed him into what appeared to be a file room. Cardboard file boxes were stacked up to the ceiling against three of the four walls. The fourth wall housed the electrical box and a shelf with three small TV monitors.

"So you didn't catch them?" Joe asked.

Con laughed bitterly. "Not even close. We had the helicopter up in the sky, we had K-9 units out with dogs. They disappeared without a trace."

Joe told Con about the redheaded man and how he'd vanished as well.

"Do you think any one of the guys could've been Meredith?" Frank asked.

"That's another strange thing," Con said, going over to the monitors. "We checked on Meredith on our way back into town. He was cleaning the courthouse, as he was supposed to be."

"Who told you that?" Joe asked.

"Judge Hopkins," Con replied. "He was watching Meredith vacuum his office carpet. You don't get a much better alibi than that."

"No, I guess not," Joe said. "Maybe he sat this one out, you know? He let his partners run this job because we were getting too close to him."

"Maybe," Frank said. "There's still too much we don't know."

Con pushed some buttons under the monitors. "Here's one more chance for some answers," he said. "These are the surveillance tapes. I'm winding them back twenty minutes."

Con pushed a few more buttons, and soon Frank and Joe were watching themselves on TV. They saw the redheaded man come in waving his gun. They saw the customers fall to the floor. They saw Frank enter first, then Joe and Biff. They saw the gunshot shatter Biff's bat. They saw the fight in the parking lot. Then it was over.

"Not much we can use," Con said, clearly disappointed.

"Wait a second," Joe said. "Rewind it to the beginning, will you?"

Con punched a button, waited, then hit Play.

The film ran for less than fifteen seconds before Joe shouted to freeze it.

Con hit Pause.

Joe was so excited he could barely talk. "Look right here," he said. He pointed to a customer at the front of the line.

Frank recognized a tall woman with light hair. "It's Sylvia," he said. "I can't believe we didn't see her."

"There was too much going on," Joe said. "Now watch what happens."

They ran through the entire film again. When the redheaded man came in, Sylvia dropped to the floor with all the others. She remained down with the others during the fight. When the Hardys chased the robber out of the bank, all the customers except one stayed down on the floor.

Only Sylvia calmly stood up, brushed herself off, and walked out the front door.

10 The Change-up

"Talk about cool as a cucumber!" Joe exclaimed. "She was never worried at all."

"I think we need to have another talk with Miss van Loveren," Con said. "She might be the inside contact after all."

Frank hated to admit it, but it seemed Con and his brother were right. He'd been wrong about Sylvia. She was guilty.

Con's walkie-talkie crackled to life. Through the static, a voice said, "Unit twelve calling unit seven. Unit twelve calling unit seven."

Con held the radio to his mouth. "This is unit seven. Go ahead."

"This is a follow-up on one Earl Galatin," the voice said. "The suspect put down the Bay View

Motel as his address on the rental car application. Checked it out. It's a dead end. Over."

"Got it," Con said. "Unit seven out."

Joe shook his head. "These guys are pretty slippery."

"They'll make a mistake," Frank said. "Then we'll make them pay for it."

Con put a hand on each of the Hardy's shoulders. "You know I like having your help," he said. "But be careful, all right?"

"Always," Joe said, grinning.

Con looked at Frank. "Make sure you keep this hardheaded brother of yours under control, okay?"

Frank smiled. "Always."

Outside, the Hardys ran into Bayport Savings' president, Alex Stendahl.

"Hold up. Hey, Jim Harper, just the person I wanted to talk to," he said as he hurried over to Joe. He looked over at Frank. "Are you a reporter for the *Globe*, too?"

"Ah, not exactly," Frank said. "Sometimes I help Jim with his . . . investigations."

"Good," Stendahl said. "Listen. The police won't tell me what happened. Was it the same guy as at Bayport Savings? Did they catch him?"

"No, he got away," Joe said.

Stendahl self-consciously touched the bandage over his eye. "Hmm. That's bad," he said.

"They're going to arrest Miss van Loveren, though, right? I mean, I saw her come out of the bank during the robbery. I know she was there."

"You saw her?" Frank asked.

"Sure." Stendahl pointed diagonally across the street. "I was sitting in my office. She came out the front door here. A few minutes later police were all over the place. That's how I knew there'd been another robbery."

"Did you see which way she went?" Joe asked.

"I certainly did. She ran down the street in that direction." Stendahl pointed up the street in the general direction of Sylvia's neighborhood. "Then she kind of disappeared."

Frank and Joe looked at each other. "Thanks," Joe said. "I'll get all this into the article I write, okay?"

"Great, great," Stendahl said. Then he lowered his voice. "Can I ask a favor?"

Joe shrugged. "It depends."

"I think I have a right to know what's happening," he whispered. He touched the bandage on his forehead again. "After all, the thief could've killed me. If you could just let me know how the police are doing. You know, if they're close to arresting anyone. It would really ease my mind."

"I'll think about it," Joe replied.

"Fine," Stendahl said. "That's all I ask." He turned and strode briskly back toward Bayport Savings.

"I wonder if that busybody thinks he's being helpful?" Frank asked.

"Who knows." Joe led the way down the street to where the van was parked.

"We've got two choices," Joe said, getting into the driver's seat. "Pay Sylvia another visit, or follow up this Earl Galatin lead."

Frank reached over his shoulder for his seat-belt strap. Out of the corner of his eye, he thought he saw something move in the back of the van. He tried to stay cool. He wanted to catch the stowaway by surprise.

As Joe pulled out into traffic, Frank signaled to his brother by tilting his head slightly toward the back.

Joe understood immediately. He kept driving. "I don't know what we should do," he said in a normal voice. "Maybe go home and go over all the evidence in detail."

"That sounds good," Frank said. At that moment he signaled Joe again.

In perfect synchronization, Joe slammed on the brakes while Frank twisted and jumped from his seat, ready to deck whoever was hiding in back.

The sudden change in momentum caused the person to fly forward. Frank held out his forearm. The person slammed into it, then bounced backward onto the floor of the van with a loud *oomph!*

Joe slammed the van into Park. "You get 'em, Frank?"

"Yeah," Frank said. He watched the person roll around on the floor, gasping for breath. "It's Sylvia," he said.

Frank helped her to get up and sit on a big soda cooler. "Sorry," he said. "You all right?"

Sylvia spoke in a halting voice. "Got . . . the . . . wind . . . knocked . . . out," she said.

"Now it's our turn to ask why you broke into *our* place," Joe said when Sylvia had caught her breath.

"I had to talk to you," Sylvia said. "I was in Empire Federal when the robbery went down."

"We know," Frank said. "We saw you on videotape."

Joe crossed his arms in front of his chest. "Why'd you take off?"

"I knew the police would see the tape and decide that I had something to do with it," Sylvia said. "I had to get out of there before they arrested me."

"We could take you to the cops right now," Joe said.

"But I know you'll at least listen to me," Sylvia said. "Remember I said I was coming downtown this afternoon to resign from Bayport Savings?"

Frank nodded.

Sylvia still held one arm over her stomach.

"That's what I did," she said. "I closed out my bank account, too. The only reason I was in Empire Federal was to deposit my money there." With her free hand she reached into her pocketbook and handed Frank a cashier's check made out in her name. "I was waiting in line when the robbery happened, that's all."

Joe didn't believe her. "That's a good cover," he said. "Very professional."

Sylvia looked as though she was going to cry. "Here," she said. She fished around in her purse some more. She handed Frank a black matchbook. "The thief dropped it when you were fighting," she said. "It landed right by my cheek, so I hid it under my hand until you chased him out."

Frank held the matchbook up. It read "Hôtel des Alpes: Genève." "Switzerland," he said. "That's where Dad is. You mind if I keep this?"

Sylvia shook her head. "Give it to the police if you think it will help. They'll take it seriously coming from you."

"Where should we drop you off?" Frank asked.

"My car's still in the Bayport Savings lot," Sylvia answered.

"We can't drop her off at her car!" Joe said in disbelief. "She's up to her neck in this, Frank."

"You're not going to skip the country, are you?" Frank asked Sylvia.

"No. I wasn't planning to."

"See," Frank said. "We know where to find her if we get proof she's involved."

"You mean *when* we get proof," Joe said. "This is a big mistake, Frank."

Despite Joe's objections, Frank nudged Joe over and climbed behind the wheel. He dropped Sylvia off at her car.

"I still can't believe you did that," Joe grumbled. He watched Sylvia scoot off in her silver-colored sports car.

"Don't blow a gasket," Frank said as they pulled out of the lot. "I want to check out the Bay View Motel, where the rental car company said Galatin was staying. I've got a hunch—about something Dad told you on the phone."

"And . . ."

"Hold on. I'll let you know when we get there."

Ten minutes later the Hardys pulled into a rundown motel along the highway overlooking the bay.

Frank led the way into the office. There, behind the desk, was a man reading a magazine. A fan on the counter blew full blast, but the little room was still boiling hot.

"Excuse me," Frank said. "We're looking for a guy who's supposed to be staying here. His name's Earl Galatin."

"The police were in here a while ago asking about that name," the man said. "I told them, and I'll tell you—I never heard of him."

"You mind if we look over your register?"

"Now, you know I can't let you do that," the old man said. "Got to protect the privacy of my guests."

"Sure," Frank said. "I understand. How about this, though? Did anybody pay in cash lately—counterfeit cash?"

The old man scowled. "How'd you know? My wife just come from the bank. She's real upset."

"Do you have any idea who passed you those bills?" Joe asked.

The man nodded. He reached under the counter and pulled up a registration book. "I figure I got a good idea." He ran his finger down the list of names. "That's him, right there," he said, turning the book so Frank could see.

Frank read the name out loud. "Larry Gainy."

"Larry Gainy?" Joe said. "That's the guy Dad talked about. His real name's Herve DuBois." He blew out a long breath. "So, that's the hunch you had that you were going to tell me about. How'd you know?"

"I didn't, until now," Frank said. "I thought Galatin might rent the car and the motel room under different names, but I had no idea it'd turn out to be this Larry Gainy, or DuBois, character."

100

"The matchbook from Switzerland," Joe said. "Now that makes sense, too. We've got to call Dad and let him know that Larry Gainy is here in Bayport!"

Frank nodded. He handed the register back to the man. "You mind if we take a look in his room?"

"The rascal checked out this morning." The man handed Frank a key. "I don't figure he left anything in there."

The Hardys headed for Room 116, down at the far end of the motel.

Frank worked the key into the lock, and Joe peeked in the window. The curtains were drawn tight.

"Stupid lock's stuck," Frank said.

Joe had his face right up to the window. Suddenly the curtains parted. There was a face, inches away, staring back at him!

11 Death from Above

"Whoa!" Joe reeled backward. The face disappeared behind the curtains. "Frank! There's someone in there!"

Frank took a quick step away from the door. "You recognize who it was?"

"No, it happened too quick."

"Hey, you two! You two fellows!" It was the front desk man, ambling down the walk from the office. "I forgot to warn you about Helen."

"Helen?" Joe said.

"The housekeeper," the man said. "Is she in there?" He went right up to Room 116 and rapped on the door.

Slowly, the door opened about eight inches. A timid face peeped out. "Yes?"

Frank guffawed. "Hi, Helen," he said. "I don't know who was more scared, you or my brother, Joe."

Joe blushed. "Hi. Sorry I frightened you."

The girl opened the door all the way. "It's okay," she said. "I'm almost finished cleaning the room. Give me ten minutes and it'll be ready for you."

"Oh, no," Frank said. "We're not staying."

"We were looking for the guy who stayed here before," Joe added. "Did you get a look at him?"

"Sure. He was a little shorter than you," Helen said, nodding toward Joe. "Wavy black hair, kind of a movie star type. You know, that's what I thought he was."

Joe raised an eyebrow. "A movie star?"

Helen giggled. "Well, not a star exactly. I know a star wouldn't stay here at the Bay View. But an actor, because of all the wigs and stuff."

"Wigs?"

"Yeah, you know those Styrofoam heads that people use to hold their wigs? I saw two of those in his room when I cleaned it yesterday—a blond one and a real bushy red one."

Joe looked at Frank. "The redheaded man! It was Herve DuBois."

"Yeah," Frank said. "And Larry Gainy and Earl Galatin all in one."

Helen looked confused.

"You've been a big help," Frank said to both Helen and the man. "Thanks."

That night, after dinner, Frank asked his mother for their father's number in Switzerland.

"I already talked to him today," she said, as Frank handed her a stack of dishes. "He's on his way home."

"He is? When?"

"He'll be back sometime tomorrow afternoon. Did you need to talk to him?"

"Tomorrow's fine," Frank said. "It can wait until then." He brought the rest of the dirty dishes in from the table, then went to find Joe.

He found his brother upstairs, sitting at his desk. He had all the map photos Phil had printed out for them laid out in order.

"Mom said Dad'll be home tomorrow," Frank said. "Maybe we should wait and show him what we've got."

Joe had his chin resting in his palm. "Maybe," he said absently.

Frank pulled up a chair. "Let's go over everything."

Joe leaned back. "We know at least three of them already, possibly four."

Frank ticked the names off on his fingers. "Bart Meredith, his cellmate Eddie Racine, and now Herve DuBois. Who's number four?"

"Sylvia."

Frank ticked off a forth finger. "Okay, she could be the one giving them inside security information. That means we're still missing somebody."

"How do you figure?"

"Herve DuBois tried to rob Empire Federal today. We know that because of the red wig in the motel room," Frank said.

Joe nodded.

"We also know that Meredith sat this one out—he was in the courthouse. That leaves the two men who staged the false alarm at the other Empire branch."

"One of them would be Eddie Racine," Joe said. "You're right. We've got one more suspect to identify."

"It's got to be Ron Quick," Frank said. "He's missing all of a sudden. The crooks are hanging out at his junkyard . . ."

"Yeah," Joe said. "He's got money troubles *and* there's that expensive copy machine in his office. He could even have been driving the black sedan when we almost got turned into a steel pancake."

"That leaves two questions," Frank said. "How do these dudes keep disappearing into thin air? And why would an international counterfeiter like Herve DuBois suddenly start pulling off bank robberies here in Bayport?"

Joe traced a finger along the lines of the video

prints. "It's got to have something to do with these maps."

"Follow the highlighter," Frank suggested.

Joe dragged his finger along the orange highlighter that someone had traced over the mysterious yellow lines. "It goes out from the junkyard in two directions," he said. "Toward downtown one way, and then right off the map into the bay in the other direction." He found another orange line and traced it. "This one goes from downtown all the way up north to where the map ends."

"But look," Frank pointed out. "The single yellow line forks into six branches just before it goes off the map. This map is incomplete."

Joe pointed to an orange question mark next to the branches. "Whoever marked it wants to know where these branches lead as much as we do."

"Hang on." Frank left the room for a minute, then returned with a regular street map of Bayport. He opened it up next to the schematic. "I think those yellow lines go to the reservoir," he said. "I have an idea. Let's mark the locations of all the robberies and false alarms."

"Grand Boulevard and State Street are already scratched on here," Joe said.

Frank pinpointed the corner of Grand and State on the street map. "Wait a minute!" he said. "That's the corner where Bayport Savings is!"

"Now we're getting somewhere."

uni-ball vision rule

Frank looked up the addresses of First City Bank and the two Empire Federal branches while Joe traced out the exact corresponding spot on the utility map.

"It matches up," Joe said, his voice hoarse with excitement. "There's a little orange dot at each of those addresses."

Frank saw where the marks were. "The targets have both been downtown," he said. "DuBois and his gang deliberately set off a false alarm at a bank on the outskirts of town while the real robbery was going on downtown."

"A great way to make sure the cops get there late," Joe noted.

Frank hovered over the map. "See any more orange dots? They could tell us where they're planning to strike next."

The Hardys searched the maze of multicolored lines carefully.

"Here!" Joe almost shouted. He had his finger out toward the western edge of the blueprints. "Can you find this spot on the street map?"

Frank measured distances from landmarks they were sure of. "The closest I can guess is that it's the corner of Arbor Avenue and Edwards."

Joe pulled a phone book from his desk. He flipped it open to banks. He ran his index finger down the listings. "Yes. There's a branch of New England National right at that corner."

"Okay," Frank said. "It's far from downtown.

If the thieves follow their pattern, that means it'll be a false alarm."

Joe eyeballed the blueprints again. "No more dots downtown," he said. "We know where the third false alarm will be, but what's the real target?"

The Hardys worked on this problem for a while. There were several banks with downtown offices, but there was no way to tell which one might be the target. Finally, after midnight, they decided to sleep on it.

The next morning Frank woke up thinking about the baseball game he was scheduled to pitch that night. He'd dreamed that he'd pitched a no-hitter, and he hoped it was a good sign.

Forcing himself out of bed, he placed a call to Con Riley at the police station. He explained the hunch he and Joe had about all the real targets being downtown and all the false alarms being on the outskirts of town.

"I'm impressed," Con said. "Good work. I'll tell Chief Collig."

After a quick breakfast, the Hardys decided to drive out to Ron's Salvage again.

"I think the key may be in the missing parts of the blueprints," Frank said, as he gunned the van down Route 6. "We need to know why there's a question mark right where the yellow lines branch out and go off the map."

Joe nodded in agreement. "Slow down," he said. "Don't get too close to the gate."

Frank pulled the van over to the shoulder of the road, and they got out.

"Whew," Joe said, pulling on his sticky T-shirt. "It's going to be another hot one."

They came to the chain-link gate. A heavy padlock hung from the lock. There didn't seem to be any activity inside.

Joe went over the fence first. He jogged over to a stack of compacted cars, then beckoned for Frank to follow. "It's clear," he whispered.

Once Frank dropped over, the Hardys crouched low and approached the office like marines assaulting an enemy stronghold.

Frank noticed that the big crane had moved. It squatted at the corner of the garage side of the office building. The disk-shaped electromagnet hung above a two-story stack of compacted cars.

The Hardys stopped outside the door and listened. Dead quiet.

Joe pulled out his lock pick, and within seconds they were in.

The place looked exactly as it had before. The desks and chairs were in the same places, and the color copier still sat against the back wall.

"Let's look for anything that might be connected to counterfeiting," Frank said. "Anything that might tell us what the next target will be."

Joe went to the desk where they'd found the first set of blueprints. He found nothing new.

Frank flipped through the contents of the file cabinets. "Man," he said. "Ron Quick owed a lot of people money. I see a whole lot of bills here but hardly any receipts."

Joe jimmied the door that led to the garage. He let out a whistle. "Hey, Frank. Take a look at this."

Frank hurried over.

Joe pointed to the body of a car sitting up on jack stands. "A nineteen thirty-two Ford," Joe said. "This baby's going to be quite a hot rod some day." He went over and ran his hand across the gleaming red paint. A small-block V-8 engine hung from a lift next to the car.

"It's great, Joe, but it isn't what we're looking for," Frank said with annoyance in his voice.

Frank turned and went back into the office while Joe stayed to admire the hot rod a little longer. He inspected the engine. Everything was chromed—the valve covers, the air cleaner, the braided brake lines. It was beautiful!

Joe jumped when he heard the rumble of an engine coming to life. At first he thought it was right inside the garage with him it was so loud. Then he realized the noise came from outside.

He sprinted from the garage to the office. "Frank!" he yelled.

The office door stood open. Through the doorway, Joe could see Frank standing out front in the gravel drive.

It was the crane. That was the engine he'd heard start up. "Frank!" he called out in warning.

He looked up and saw the boom start to move. The huge disk magnet, carrying a compacted car, swung directly over Frank's head.

12 Blueprint for Disaster

Joe knew that as soon as he stopped hearing the hum of the electromagnet, the compacted car would plummet to earth.

He rushed toward his brother. In one tiny instant, he saw Frank's expression change from confusion to fear, and he heard the hum of the magnet cut off. Joe knew the car was now falling, but he also knew he didn't have time to look up. He had to trust that he would get to Frank before the two-ton hunk of steel crushed them both like bugs.

He hit Frank low as he lifted him with his legs and shoulders. His brother went flying.

Joe crashed to the ground on his belly and slid as if he were going in to home plate. Even before he stopped skidding, he heard the compacted car slam into the ground behind him.

They were safe!

Joe heard the electromagnet crackle back to life. He'd spoken too soon—they weren't safe yet.

"Joe, get up!" It was Frank.

Joe got up in time to see the boom of the crane swing back over the stack of cars. The disk magnet dropped down and pulled one of the autos up to it as easily as a vacuum cleaner sucks up a speck of dirt.

The boom swung back out over the Hardys.

"Split up!" Joe shouted. He sprinted to hide behind a row of junked cars.

The humming stopped again, and Joe felt the ground shake as a solid square of metal fell to the earth only inches behind him. He dove to the ground, hunkering down behind a flattened minivan.

Then, suddenly, the crane engine shut down.

Joe peeked out from his hiding place. He saw his brother do the same from across the way.

They both crept out into the open. Whoever had been in the cab of the crane was now gone.

"Where in the world . . ." Joe muttered.

Going up to the crane, Frank came across the storm drain Joe had tripped over during their first run-in with Bart Meredith. Lying next to it in the dust was a long crowbar like the one the redheaded man had used to crack him in the shin.

"Joe," he said. "I think I know how our suspects have been dropping out of sight so quickly."

Joe came over. "How?"

Frank picked up the crowbar. Its flattened tip fit perfectly into a notch in the rim of the drain's lid. With hardly any effort at all, Frank was able to pry the lid up and shove it aside.

Joe stared down into the darkness. "They've been escaping into the sewers? That's nasty!"

Frank sat down and swung his feet into the opening. "Not the sewers, Joe. These are the storm drains." Reaching in with his left hand, Frank found the top rung of a ladder. He climbed down into the darkness.

Joe reluctantly followed.

Once they got to the bottom of the ladder, Frank and Joe found themselves in a cement pipe wide enough to drive a car through. They waded through water about eighteen inches deep. Soon the light from the opening above was too faint to illuminate the tunnel. Frank dug his penlight out of his jeans pocket. It barely made enough light for them to see each other's faces.

"Storm drains?" Joe asked. His voice echoed in the cavern.

"Yeah," Frank said. "They have nothing to do

with the pipes that take dirty water back to the sewage treatment plant. They catch storm water and carry it to the bay so the streets don't flood."

"That's got to be why the first bank robber disappeared on that videotape," Joe said. "While the camera was focused on the other side of the parking lot, he dropped down into a storm drain."

"You got it," Frank said. "And Herve DuBois did the same thing in the middle of the alley."

"Then where do they go? I'd get lost in here."

Frank held up his fist. "That's it, Joe! You figured it out."

"Huh?"

Frank slapped his brother on the shoulder. "The yellow lines on the blueprints—they represent these storm drains. They're using the blueprints to get around under here."

Joe grinned. "I knew I'd get the answer sooner or later." He waded back toward the entrance. Frank's penlight threw an orange glow off the rippling water.

They climbed out and pushed the lid back in place. "It would take hours to walk downtown through those drains," Joe said. "Even if you did have a map."

Frank rose up on his toes, making water squish out of his sneakers. "Yeah," he said. "Walking wouldn't make sense." He rubbed the back of his neck in thought. "I don't know," he said finally.

"I also want to know where they got those blueprints," Joe said.

Frank smiled. "Joe, you genius, you're two for two now."

Joe had come to the answer at the same time as his brother. "The courthouse!"

"And who do we know who sometimes works in the courthouse?"

"Bart Meredith," Joe said.

Frank checked his watch. "Let's pay a visit to our favorite janitor."

Back in the van Joe took out the cell phone as Frank sped toward the center of town. "I'm giving Biff a call," he said. "After the tip he gave us yesterday, he deserves to see Meredith go down."

"Tell him to be outside his house," Frank said. "I'll swing by and pick him up."

Biff was ready and waiting. Joe popped the latch on the sliding door, and Biff hopped in before the van had even stopped. He sat down in back.

"We're going after the moron who ran me off the road?" he asked with excitement.

Joe nodded. "It could get rough."

"I didn't think you were inviting me to a tea party," Biff replied.

A minute or so later Frank slowed down. He found a parking spot about half a block down from the courthouse. He eased past it, then put the van in reverse to parallel park.

"Wait," Joe said, putting his hand on the steering wheel. "Is that him?"

Frank squinted out the windshield. A big guy in dark green coveralls had come out of the courthouse and was going down the steps two at a time. He was carrying a long cardboard tube under his arm. Frank watched as he turned his head, flipping his long ponytail over his shoulder. "It's him," he said.

"Hurry, Frank," Joe said. "Pull up. We'll jump out and give him a little surprise."

Frank did nothing.

Meredith climbed into the same car they'd seen him in that first night—a rusted-out blue two-door coupe.

Joe pounded the dashboard with his fist. "Come on, Frank! He'll get away."

Meredith drove off, leaving a cloud of exhaust.

Frank pulled out. "Patience, Joe. Let's tail him and see where he's going in such a hurry."

They wove through traffic, staying five or six car lengths back to keep from tipping the ex-con off.

"He's headed north," Biff said.

Frank nodded. "I think he's going to the reservoir."

Sure enough, five minutes later, they watched

as Meredith came to the bridge spanning Bayport's manmade lake.

Instead of going over the bridge, Meredith slowed almost to a stop and turned onto a narrow blacktop road.

"That road loops all the way around the reservoir," Biff said.

After waiting a minute or so to give Meredith a head start, Frank swung the van onto the blacktop. To the left, he could see a thick forest of tall trees. Their branches hung out over the road, shading it from the sun. To the right was a steep slope running down about fifty feet to the water.

Frank drove slowly, letting Meredith disappear around each corner in front of them before following. He watched the odometer. When they'd traveled a little over half a mile, he saw the reservoir dam rise up on the horizon. It was a sheer face of white concrete.

Frank knew from the picnics he and his family had had out here that on the far side of the dam the water rose almost to the top. On this side, the city kept the water level much lower, exposing at least sixty feet of the face of the dam.

"Watch it, Frank. He's pulling over." Joe turned to Biff. "See my binoculars back there, buddy?"

When Frank had pulled over into the weeds, Biff handed up a pair of powerful field glasses.

Joe rolled his window down and scoped the

scene. A big green blur filled the lenses. Joe rotated the focus knob and the dam became suddenly clear, filling his field of vision.

A narrow catwalk ran the length of the dam on the side facing them. A ladder extended down fifty or sixty feet to the water. Sluiceways at the base of the dam poured water into the reservoir like giant faucets. The force of the spray churned the lake there into white foam.

Joe tried to focus on the spot where the dam met the shore on the near side of the reservoir. "I can't see Meredith," he said. "We need to get closer."

The Hardys and Biff quietly exited the van. They crept along, hidden in the weeds and grass. "Careful not to step over the edge," Frank whispered. "It's a long way down to the water."

They stopped a few yards behind Meredith's car. From here they could see everything.

Meredith had walked out to the middle of the catwalk. A stocky guy stepped out of a service door at the top of the dam.

"Who's that?" Biff asked.

Joe looked through the binoculars. He immediately recognized the crook he'd picked out of the mug books. "Eddie Racine," he said. "Meredith's cellmate in prison."

They could hear voices, but couldn't make out the words. "I think they're arguing," Frank said. He watched as Meredith opened up the cardboard tube and removed some rolled-up papers. He grabbed the field glasses from Joe. "We were right!" Frank said. "He's got more blueprints."

Biff pointed down to the foot of the dam. "Hey man, what kind of crazy thing is going on down there?"

A paved boat ramp curved steeply down from the blacktop road to the foot of the dam.

"That's the truck from Ron's Salvage!" Joe exclaimed.

Joe was right. A white pickup with a trailer attached had backed down all the way to the water. Bobbing next to the trailer was a red- and white-striped wave-runner—a waterjet-powered craft with motorcycle-style seat and controls.

"The wave-runner's basically floating free," Joe said. "Looks like somebody's in the middle of unloading it from the trailer."

"I was, until I got interrupted!" a voice boomed from behind them.

Biff and the Hardys spun around. A wiry guy with brown hair parted in the middle and tattoos covering his arms stood there grinning.

He pulled a wicked-looking hunting knife from a sheath on his belt.

"Get going," he ordered, stabbing the air with the blade. "Out on the catwalk, now!"

Biff led the way out onto the walkway. Frank was next, followed by Joe and the thug.

As the Hardys and Biff got close to Meredith and Racine, it became even more obvious to Frank that the men were arguing about something. Now is our chance, Frank thought. It was three against three, and Meredith and Racine were too busy shouting to know what was going on.

Frank held three fingers behind his back for Joe to see. With each second, he folded one back into his fist, indicating the ticking off of seconds.

Joe knew the signal. When Frank got to zero, Joe spun, smashing his forearm onto the thug's wrist. The knife flew free, spinning down into the water below.

Frank pushed Biff forward. The two of them charged Meredith and his pal.

Joe threw a right hook into Tattoo's gut. The guy doubled over with a grunt. Bending his knees for leverage, Joe went for a left uppercut.

His fist caught nothing but air. The crook had bobbed to the side just enough. For a split second, Joe was almost off balance.

He stepped back and felt only wide open space. He grabbed for the rail. It was too late. He watched the catwalk recede as he fell. He plummeted backward—helpless—toward the boiling foam at the bottom of the dam.

13 The Third Strike

Meredith and Racine were running away—the cowards, Frank thought. Racine tried to jump up from the catwalk to the top of the dam, while Meredith sprinted for the far side of the reservoir.

Frank stopped and climbed up on the railing of the catwalk to reach the top of the dam. He'd go after Racine and let Biff have Meredith.

The thick-necked thug had scrambled up to the top of the dam and was trying to make his way like a tightrope walker back to the shore.

Frank was reaching up to grab at Racine's ankle when he heard a bloodcurdling scream.

He spun in time to see his brother plunge into the roiling foam below. "Joe!" he shouted.

He waited a few seconds. "Come up, Joe," he

pleaded. "Come up for air." Joe didn't surface. All Frank could see was the bubbling water.

Frank went for the ladder leading down the face of the dam. Racine and the tattooed thug were sprinting free toward the shore, but Frank didn't care. He had to save Joe!

He swung onto the ladder, almost slipping off. Descending quickly, he kept one eye on the water, the other on the slick ladder rungs. He didn't see Joe anywhere. He must still be underwater, Frank thought. He wasn't sure how many seconds had passed—thirty, forty—how long could Joe last?

Finally he reached the bottom rung. The water splashed and bubbled all around him. He couldn't see anything, and he could only guess at how deep it was. If he jumped in, he'd be sucked under just as his brother had been.

He glanced toward the far shore. Meredith had scrambled down the steep muddy bank and was standing by the water. Biff was sliding down behind him. Frank saw Biff throw a punch. Meredith ducked, then dove into the water.

What was going on?

Frank scanned the reservoir. The water became calm about fifty yards out from the dam. There! What was that? Was it Joe?

Frank saw a head bob to the surface in the center of the lake. Joe appeared to be unconscious.

Then Frank realized why Meredith had dove in. He was swimming toward Joe. He was swimming out to finish Joe off!

His heart pounding, Frank rushed back up the ladder two rungs at a time. He had to get to a place where it was safe to dive in. He had to get to Joe before Meredith did.

Frank sprinted the length of the catwalk. Glancing down at the water, he saw Meredith stroking out powerfully. He was mere yards from Joe.

Frank made it to the end of the dam and ran down the ridge, finding a place to scuttle down the embankment. His foot caught on a root and he pitched forward, rolling, bouncing, tumbling down. He skidded to a stop at the edge of the water.

He jumped up, ready to dive in. Something held him back. It was Biff, his big hand on Frank's shoulder.

He followed Biff's gaze out over the water. There was Meredith, his arm around Joe's chest in the classic lifesaving position, sidestroking in to shore.

When Meredith got close, Frank and Biff helped lift Joe from the water. Frank slapped his brother on the cheek. "Joe! Joe!"

Joe coughed. His eyes opened. "Frank? What happened? I fell, I think. . . ."

"You're okay," Frank said. "Meredith pulled you out."

Meredith had flopped down on the bank, soaking and exhausted. He gasped for breath.

"Thanks," Frank said.

Meredith was so tired he could only hold his hand up as if to say, You're welcome.

"What's the deal, Meredith?" Frank asked, helping Joe sit up. "You didn't have to help my brother."

Meredith finally caught his breath. "I told you, man. I turned my life around."

"You mean you're not part of this gang?" Frank asked.

"No," Meredith said. "They tricked me."

"Tricked you?" Biff asked.

Meredith shook the water from his long hair and retied his ponytail. "Those two," he said, referring to Racine and the tattooed man. "Eddie Racine and Bobby Knapp, I knew them in prison. They told me they had a legitimate business going. Construction, they said."

Meredith stared out over the water. "I don't want to be a janitor for the rest of my life, so I said I wanted in. They asked me to get some special blueprints from the courthouse."

Frank nodded. "They show all the utilities."

"Right," Meredith said. "I started to feel like they were blowing smoke, though, because they

125

wouldn't tell me why they needed the maps. That's what me and Racine were fighting about."

"Are they working with anybody else?" Frank asked.

Meredith nodded. "There's one other dude I know of. He's got dark hair. Larry Gainy's his name."

Or Herve DuBois, Frank thought to himself.

"He was the one with the money," Meredith said. "He paid me six bills for those prints, but I lost my wallet."

Frank reached into his back pocket. "Is this it?" he asked, tossing the wallet to Bart.

"Hey, thanks, man."

"Bad news, though," Joe said, standing up. "Those hundreds are fakes."

Meredith's upper lip curled in anger. He removed the bills and examined them. "Oh, man! I'll kill him. I can't believe it!"

"You'd better steer clear of your old pals from now on," Frank said. "We think they're using those maps to plan bank robberies."

Meredith looked scared. "And I helped them without even knowing it. This is bad, man. I'm in big trouble."

"Maybe Frank and I can help," Joe said. "Let us have a look at that latest set of maps you brought for them and we'll talk to the cops about what you did here today."

"Hey, that'd be cool," Meredith said. "I dropped the stuff up on the bank there."

The four of them climbed up. Joe looked across the reservoir. Both the pickup and the wave-runner were gone. He wondered what the crooks were using the wave-runner for. They were fun for zipping around on—jumping wakes and stuff—but they weren't very good for anything else.

Meredith found the papers in the grass and unrolled them. Then he used rocks to pin down each corner.

Frank immediately recognized these pages as the ones missing from the first set he and Joe had found. "Here," he said to Joe. "Here's where the yellow line branches out and disappears on the first maps we saw. On these you can see that they all lead to different parts of the reservoir. You can tell which storm drain leads directly from the dam to downtown."

"Did you give Racine a copy of these?" Joe asked.

"Yeah," Meredith said. "He grabbed it out of my hand when you guys came after us."

"So they have everything they need to pull another heist," Frank said. He studied the map. "We know the next false alarm is going to be at the suburban branch of New England National, but we don't know which downtown bank is really going to get hit."

"Unless . . ." Joe said. "Unless it's not a bank at all."

Biff crossed his arms. "What do you mean?"

Joe looked at Frank. "Dad said Herve DuBois stole the special ink used for U.S. currency. A month ago, somebody got hold of the printing plates at the mint. What else do you need for perfect counterfeiting?"

Frank remembered what Sylvia had said. "The micro-coded paper!"

"And Sylvia said they store it right here in Bayport. That's got to be the next target!"

Frank scanned the maps, "Okay, okay, but where would you store something so important?" He held his finger over the middle of downtown Bayport, then moved it half an inch, to where he thought the very end of State Street would be. "The Federal Armory," he said, pointing. "Of course! They'd store it at the Federal Armory. There's a yellow line going right under it."

"They're going to hit it and use the storm drain to escape, like before," Joe said.

Frank rolled up the maps. "We've got to tell Con," he said.

The Hardys and Biff jogged back to the van, while Meredith got into his rusted car. He said he had to change clothes and get back to work. Frank and Joe promised to explain his situation to the police.

Joe held his T-shirt out the window as they drove, trying to get it dry. "You think DuBois will try to hit the armory today?" he asked.

"I don't know," Frank replied. "There's been a robbery each of the past two days, though. It would fit the pattern."

"Think the police will listen to us?" Biff asked.

Joe pulled his shirt back in and put it on. "They'd better," he said.

The tires squealed as Frank whipped into the police station.

The three friends ran inside, only to be stopped by the desk sergeant.

"Stop right there!" he said. "Who are you here to see?"

Con Riley stepped out into the hallway. "It's okay," he said, waving Biff and the Hardys forward.

They joined Con in the Situation Room, where at least ten other officers sat waiting.

"I told Chief Collig about your theory," Con said. "We've got to respond to every alarm, of course, even if we think it's a fake call. But we have officers here ready to respond to every downtown bank as soon as any call comes in."

"It's not going to be a bank," Frank said.

"What?"

Several officers turned and scowled at the three teenagers.

Frank went to a desk and unrolled the maps.

129

"We think the leader of the thieves is an international counterfeiter named Herve DuBois."

Con looked doubtful. "Why would he rob banks?"

"It's all a setup," Joe said. "They want you running all over town while they go for the real target."

"Which is?" one of the officers asked.

"The Federal Armory," Frank said.

Laughter broke out all through the room, then quickly died down as Chief Collig strode into the room.

"What's this about the armory?" he asked.

"It's the next target," Frank said. "That's where the micro-coded paper is stored. The thieves are escaping into the storm drains. That's why we haven't been able to catch them."

Now it was Chief Collig's turn to have a hearty laugh. "Storm drains? Armory? You've got to be kidding, son. The armory is crawling with armed guards. No one would dare."

He walked over to a giant wall map of Bayport. "Gentlemen," he said, addressing his officers. "We expect a false alarm to come in from the outskirts, but the *real target*," he continued, glaring at the Hardys, "will be one of the downtown banks."

Frank started to protest, but the desk sergeant ran into the room.

"We got it!" he shouted. He held up a piece of

130

paper. "We have an alarm at a branch office of New England National."

Chief Collig smiled. "That's our false alarm." He pointed at two officers. "Wiggens, Marks, go check it out. Everybody else, go to the downtown banks you've been assigned. And be careful— these men are dangerous!"

The room became a frenzy of noise and motion as all the officers got up to leave. The first ones out ran smack into another officer on his way in.

"We've got another alarm!" he shouted over the commotion.

"Where?" Collig asked.

"The downtown branch of Bayport Savings."

Collig clenched his fist in the air. "Just as I said it would happen."

Frank looked over at his brother. How could he and Joe have been so wrong?

14 Into the Maze

"Biff," Frank said. "Follow Con to Bayport Savings. If it turns out it's really being robbed, make sure he puts a man at every storm drain nearby—especially those in the parking lot."

"You got it, Frank." Biff ran out after the officers.

As quickly as the Situation Room had become a beehive of activity, it became as still and quiet as a tomb. The Hardys were left standing completely alone.

"Do you still think it's the armory?" Joe asked.

Frank paused, then nodded firmly.

"Okay, then. I say we go check it out."

Outside, the downtown streets were bristling with the signs of a dangerous situation. S.W.A.T. team snipers were perched atop the taller buildings. Black-and-white cruisers and unmarked cars blocked the entrances to all the banks. Their light-bars flashed out warnings, but the sirens were silent.

Officers stationed themselves safely behind the open cruiser doors, and sternly waved pedestrians back. Everyone seemed ready for a showdown.

Frank started up the van.

"Take the side streets," Joe said. "The police have the middle of State Street blocked off."

Frank wove slowly through back streets until they were within a block of the armory. Frank stopped the van. He took a deep breath before getting out. "Ready?"

"As I'll ever be," Joe replied.

Unlike the area just a couple of blocks away, the area around the armory was calm.

Frank waited on the street, while Joe took the cement steps two at a time up to the front door. Before he reached the top step, a young man in camouflage fatigues had opened the huge wooden door. He had a black assault rifle slung over his shoulder.

"May I help you, sir?" he asked.

Joe stopped a few feet from the soldier. "Ah, this may sound funny," he said, scratching his head. "But we—that's my brother and I—think somebody may try to rob you guys today."

The soldier grinned. "You're joking, right?"

"Ah, no. Do you mind if I speak to your commander?"

The soldier placed a hand lightly on the stock of his rifle. "I don't think he has time for this." The soldier laughed. "Thanks for your concern, though." He stepped back inside and slammed the door.

Joe headed down the steps. "He seems to think everything's okay."

"That was a pretty mean-looking rifle," Frank said. "I can see why he's not too worried."

Joe put a hand on his brother's shoulder. "I can tell *you're* still concerned."

Frank nodded. "This has to be the target. Come on. I have an idea."

Joe followed Frank back to the van.

Frank opened the rear gate and rummaged around. He pulled out a tire iron and a big flashlight. "You carry the maps," he said to Joe. "Find the nearest storm drain."

The Hardys soon came across a drain lid behind the dry cleaner next to the armory compound. Joe noticed the dry cleaner employees watching them from inside while Frank pried up the edge of the heavy cast-iron lid. "We've got an audience," he said.

"Good," Frank replied. "I work better with somebody watching." He motioned for Joe to help push the lid aside. "Okay," he said. "I'll go first." He stepped down on to the ladder and then disappeared into the darkness below the street.

Joe went next, pulling the lid closed after he was in.

It was dark as night until Frank clicked on the flashlight. The drain extended in both directions for ten or twenty yards, then branched into yet more tunnels. "Which way?" Frank whispered.

Joe sloshed over to the light and consulted the map. "Straight that way, then one branch to the left," he said, pointing behind Frank.

They had taken only a few steps, when Joe heard a noise.

"You hear that?" he asked. "It sounded like voices."

Frank nodded.

They tried not to make splashing sounds as they walked. Coming to the left-hand branch, they saw light streaming out of the tunnel. Frank killed the flashlight. They crept to the junction. Frank peeked around the corner.

He darted back quickly and grabbed Joe by the shirt. "We were right," he whispered. "Take a look for yourself."

The brothers traded places. Joe leaned forward. What he saw amazed him.

A wave-runner sat about twenty-five yards away, floating under a ragged hole in the top of the tunnel. Behind the wave-runner, chunks of rock and cement were stacked in a pile almost five feet high.

Joe turned back to Frank. "DuBois and his gang are in there right now and the armory guards don't even know it."

"It's a great plan," Frank said. "I should've figured it out when we saw the wave-runner at the reservoir. Those things only need a few inches of water."

"Yeah," Joe agreed. "A wave-runner to get around fast under here, and a jackhammer to go up through the floor. I'll bet they went directly into the vault. DuBois could've been working on that hole off and on for the past two days. No one had a clue what was going on."

Joe peered around again. "I see only one wave-runner, though. It looked like the trailer at the reservoir could hold two."

"Don't forget the false alarm at New England National," Frank said. "I'll bet the guy who set it off is already jetting back to the dam."

The voices grew louder.

Joe pulled back to keep from being seen. Slowly, cautiously, he looked around again. He watched as first one man, then another, hung from the jagged hole and dropped down into the shallow water.

"It's Herve DuBois and the tattooed guy, Bobby Knapp," he whispered to Frank.

Each man had a thick tube wrapped in plastic strapped to his back. It looked as though they were carrying three-foot-wide rolled-up carpets, but Joe knew the packages were really rolls of micro-coded paper.

The next thing the Hardys heard was the wave-runner rumbling to life.

Frank gripped the tire iron and steadied himself.

The howl of the engine grew louder. Frank made ready to swing the tire iron.

The jetcraft burbled out of the connecting tunnel, its single headlight shining a yellow square along the wall. DuBois was driving, and Knapp rode behind him. DuBois spotted the Hardys immediately. His eyes grew wide with surprise and anger. Then he steered straight at them, gunning the engine.

Frank jumped back. He pressed himself close to the cool curve of the tunnel wall.

The wave-runner rocketed past, brushing his legs and shooting out a thick arc of dirty water.

Seconds later the sound of the engine was gone. The only trace of the theft was the rippling and sloshing of the water against the storm drain walls.

Joe wiped his face. "Man, that was close." He got the map out. "They're headed back to the reservoir."

"Quiet!" Frank said. He pointed down the

tunnel in the opposite direction from where the wave-runner had gone. A yellow rectangle of light played along the walls. It gradually grew brighter.

Frank pushed Joe forward and into the connecting tunnel, where they could hide. He dried his hands on the front of his shirt and hefted the tire iron. "I'm not going to miss this time," he said.

They heard a low rumble, like a speedboat idling. "It must be our friend Eddie Racine," Joe said, "on his way back from setting off the alarm at New England National."

It didn't take long to prove Joe right. Eddie came chugging by at a leisurely pace, and as soon as he came into view, Frank clocked him with the tire iron.

Joe caught him as he fell from the wave-runner. "He's out cold," he said. Joe didn't want Racine to drown in the tunnel, so he hoisted the thug over his shoulder and, with Frank's help, pushed him up through the jackhammered hole and onto the floor of the armory vault. "There," he said. "Have a great nap."

By the time he dropped back into the drain, Frank was already on the wave-runner. Joe clambered on behind him. Frank pulled the throttle and they were off, zooming through the tunnel.

They had to stop twice for Joe to check the

blueprints, but soon Frank was sure they were getting close to the reservoir.

He cut the engine and glided around a corner. Up ahead, they saw DuBois's wave-runner. It was roped to a ladder leading up to an oversize drain cover.

Even through the thick cement walls, Frank and Joe could hear the thunder of the sluiceways above them. "We've got to be almost directly under the dam," Frank whispered as he climbed up the ladder.

With a mighty push, he lifted the drain lid up a single inch and held it there. Circling around like a submarine captain surveying the horizon with a periscope, he scanned the area above. He couldn't see much; it was dark, except for an eerie green glow.

"Looks clear," he said. "Wait a second . . . is that a chair?"

He shoved the lid out of the way and climbed out. He found himself in the control room of the dam. Generators hummed in the background. Valves and dials lined the walls, and two chairs sat next to a glowing computer console.

In the dim light, Frank recognized the shape of a man sitting in one of the chairs.

Frank jumped. "Who's there?"

The man made a grunting sound, but didn't move.

"Joe, quick! Hand up the flashlight!" Frank grabbed the light and aimed it at the chair. It was a man all right. He was older and balding, and he was bound and gagged.

"Get up here, Joe!"

"I'm up," Joe said. "What is it?"

Overhead lights flickered on. Frank spun around. A door at the far end of the control room opened and Herve DuBois stepped in, followed closely by Bobby Knapp and a tall, thin man in khaki shorts and a red knit shirt.

Joe lunged forward. "Alex Stendahl!"

In a flash, Knapp had his knife out, the blade inches from Joe's throat. Joe backed off.

Stendahl held up a hand signaling Knapp to remain calm. He eyed Joe. "If it isn't Jim Harper. Or is it *Joe Hardy?* How'd you find us here? Where's Racine?"

"He's back at the armory," Joe said bitterly. "Dreaming about printing millions in counterfeit bills."

Stendahl pursed his lips. "That means you know our plans."

Frank tried to signal Joe to keep quiet, but his brother didn't notice. "We know the bank robberies were just a cover," Joe said. "A plan to fool the police while you pulled off the real heist."

"That's enough," DuBois said. "We've got to hurry to stay on schedule."

Joe kept his eyes fixed on Stendahl. "You had

me going," he said. "I thought Sylvia set up the bank jobs, but it was you, wasn't it?"

Stendahl laughed. "Herve here made it a good show by giving me this bruise on my head during the robbery. We had the cops completely fooled. Too bad you and your brother didn't stay fooled as long as they did."

He gestured toward the man in the chair. "Since you know so much, Joe, you're in the same boat as our friend from the junkyard, Ron Quick. He's about to go for a swim, and I think you and your brother should join him."

15 Weathering the Storm

"I already had a swim today," Joe said. He brought his left forearm up, knocking Bobby Knapp's knife hand into the air. As Bobby reeled backward, Joe smashed a right into his jaw. The knife clattered to the cement floor.

Knapp's mouth leaked a trickle of blood, but he recovered his balance and came back at Joe.

Frank was on Herve DuBois in an instant. He flashed out a side kick. DuBois jumped clear. Frank stepped right into a spinning back kick. DuBois ducked.

"You're quick for such a tall kid," DuBois hissed. "But how's your defense?" He came at Frank with a windmill-like flurry of punches and kicks. Frank neatly blocked each one.

Then DuBois made a mistake. He tried a spinning backhand punch. When Frank ducked, DuBois's fist flew past and his jaw was exposed. Frank hit him with two quick rights, dropping him to the ground.

A few feet away Joe had Bobby down and was twisting one of his tattooed arms behind his back.

"Let him up!"

The voice belonged to Stendahl.

Joe looked over to see Stendahl standing behind Ron Quick. He held Bobby Knapp's knife under the scrap yard owner's chin. Joe reluctantly let Knapp scramble to his feet.

Frank stood over DuBois, his chest heaving as he tried to catch his breath.

"Over there!" Stendahl shouted, waving the blade of the knife toward Joe.

Frank unclenched his fists and walked over to stand next to his brother.

"Where's the rope?" Stendahl asked.

"I have it." DuBois left the control room for a moment before returning with a long coil of rope. He tossed the coil to Knapp. "Tie them up in the tunnel," he ordered.

Knapp gave Joe a shove. "Get on down that ladder," he growled.

When Joe hesitated, Stendahl poked Quick in the neck, drawing a tiny bead of blood. Quick yelped in pain.

143

Joe scooted into the hole.

Down in the storm drain, Bobby Knapp made Frank and Joe sit back-to-back in the water. He bound their wrists and ran the rope through the bottom rung of the ladder. A few minutes later, he brought Ron Quick down and tied him up next to Frank.

The three of them sat huddled around the bottom of the ladder.

Herve DuBois called down to them. Joe looked up. The counterfeiter's face seemed to fill the opening to the control room above.

"You're so smart," DuBois said. "Now guess what's going to happen."

Joe watched DuBois look back and make a turning motion with his hand. Then he stared down at them again.

"Stendahl is turning a few valves up here," DuBois said. He laughed. "We're going to flood the storm drain. In ten minutes you'll be completely under water."

Joe could still hear DuBois laughing even after he slammed the drain cover shut, plunging them into total darkness.

Frank felt Ron Quick shiver with fear.

"What's that noise?" Joe asked.

"Rushing water. They're sending water from the reservoir to the bay, and it's going to go right over us."

144

Joe struggled against the ropes. "We might not even have ten minutes," he said. "The water's up to my chest!"

"Be patient, Joe."

"Patient! Are you nuts?" Joe shouted.

Ron Quick made a frightened humming noise through his gag.

"I'm with him," Joe said. "This is serious!"

"No. I mean, give me time to work here," Frank said. "These ropes are made of cotton. They'll stretch when they get wet. Keep flexing your wrists under water."

The water was up to Joe's neck now, and he kept working his wrists back and forth. He thought he felt the rope give a little.

"I'm out!" Frank said. He stood up, shaking the rope free from his arms. He then knelt down and felt under the water until he was able to untie Joe and Ron.

"Oh, thank goodness." Ron sighed when his gag came off. "I've been locked up in this place for days."

"You're almost home free," Frank said.

A beam of light shot down from above.

"They're coming back," Frank whispered. "Sit down as if you're still tied up."

The drain lid opened all the way, and Stendahl descended, followed by DuBois and Knapp. They all carried big hikers' backpacks.

Frank guessed they were filled with the ingredients for counterfeiting—the plates, ink, and paper.

The Hardys and Quick sat quietly, letting the water rise slowly to their chins. They watched as Stendahl grabbed one of the wave-runners and wrestled it around so it faced the direction of the bay.

DuBois checked his watch and mumbled something about being behind schedule.

Frank leaned over and whispered in Ron's ear. "When I give the signal, you go up the ladder as fast as you can and close the hatch."

Ron nodded slightly.

"Cover it with something heavy," Frank continued. "Shut off the valves, then call the police and the coast guard. I think they're going to try to escape through the bay."

DuBois straddled his wave-runner and cranked the engine. It burbled to life. Stendahl got on behind him, while Bobby Knapp got on the second wave-runner and turned around.

The instant DuBois started forward, the Hardys exploded out of the water. They had only seconds to act.

Frank and Joe each held one end of the rope. As Bobby Knapp's wave-runner lurched into motion, the Hardys threw the coil of rope as far in front of it as they could. Just as he got up to speed, Bobby Knapp hit the rope and the Hardys yanked as hard as they could.

Knapp went flying off the back.

Before Knapp could recover, Joe chugged through the hip-deep water and grabbed the handle of the wave-runner. He jumped on. Frank got on behind him. They took off after DuBois just as Ron Quick made it to the top of the ladder and closed the sewer lid, leaving Bobby Knapp stranded in the drain.

Joe squeezed the throttle as far as it would go. The wave-runner blasted through the drain tunnel, chasing the faint gleam of DuBois's headlamp. Frank hung on for dear life.

After three or four harrowing turns and long, full-speed straightaways, the headlamp in front of them started to grow brighter.

Then it grew even brighter. And brighter.

"I think we're coming to the bay!" Frank shouted over the din of the engine.

Joe couldn't hear. "What?" he yelled.

"I think we're coming to the bay!"

The light was very, very bright now. Joe kept the throttle wide open.

Frank looked ahead. The tunnel ended! All he could see was bright blue sky.

They blasted out of the tunnel as if shot from a cannon. Frank looked down in terror. They were sailing through the air ten or fifteen feet above the gray, choppy water of the bay.

They hit the water with a deafening *smack!* Frank bounced a foot off the seat but managed to hang on.

Stendahl hadn't been so lucky. The Hardys passed him floating in the bay, using his pack to keep his head above water.

Joe kept after DuBois, now only fifty feet ahead.

Frank pointed at a speedboat anchored in the distance. "That must be his getaway vehicle!"

Joe hunkered down to cut the wind resistance. They had to keep DuBois from getting on that boat.

Joe came up alongside the fugitive, and DuBois steered away.

Joe moved up on him again. Frank jumped. He reached out as far as he could. With his fingertips, he caught the strap of the backpack and pulled with all his strength. DuBois fell from the wave-runner. He and Frank skipped across the bay like downed water-skiers.

Then it was a race for DuBois's wave-runner. It circled lazily in the water, waiting for a rider.

Without the heavy pack to slow him, it was a race Frank won easily.

He climbed on board as DuBois shouted angrily at him. Frank ignored him and steered his wave-runner up next to Joe's. "These things are fun," he said. "I wonder if we can keep them."

A few minutes later a coast guard cutter appeared on the horizon. "Hey, fellas!" Joe shouted to DuBois and Stendahl. "Here comes your ride."

At eight-thirty that night Frank and Joe were back at the baseball diamond, preparing for their game. The Hardys played catch next to the bench to warm up, while Biff strapped on his catcher's pads.

"So Sylvia van Loveren wasn't involved?" Biff asked.

"Nope," Joe said. "Stendahl tried to set her up at the Bayport Savings heist, and then she was in the wrong place at the wrong time during the Empire Federal job."

Frank practiced his curveball. His control was his strong point as a pitcher, and he wanted all his pitches working right. "Meredith didn't turn out to be such a bad guy either," he said.

A horn beeped from the parking lot.

"Who's that?" Joe asked.

Frank stopped throwing. "I don't recognize the car, do you?"

Joe shook his head. It was a new, gold-colored sedan.

A man and a woman got out of the car. The woman waved.

"Check it out," Joe said. "It's Mom and Dad. And it looks like Mom has a new car."

"Nice car, Mom!" Frank called. "When can I drive it?"

Mrs. Hardy laughed. "Never!" she shouted back. "Not after what happened last time."